**"I have som**   D1622909

"What?"

He pulled something from the pocket of his pale blue scrubs—a pair of rumpled tickets. Cassidy recognized the insignia on them instantly. Her mouth fell open. "The skating rink! You remembered."

"Of course I remembered. You said you wanted to go skating the night the ice rink opened in George Square, so I bought us some tickets."

She stared at the tickets. There it was again. Just when everything in her head was giving her lots of reasons to end this relationship, just when she hadn't been alone with him for a few days and felt as though she was starting to shake him out of her system, he did something like this.

Something thoughtful. Something kind. Something that would matter only to her. He'd even managed to plan ahead—a trait distinctly lacking in most men she knew.

"So are we going to capture the spirit of Christmas?" he whispered in her ear.

One look from those big blue eyes and he was instantly back in her system. Like a double-shot espresso. "You betcha." She smiled at him.

Dear Reader,

Christmas is my absolute favorite time of year. I spend every Christmas Eve praying for some snow to fall and hoping we'll get a white Christmas. I love putting up my Christmas tree, wrapping presents, watching Christmas films and, most of all, I love to see Christmas-themed books on the shelves—so much so that I begged my editor to let me write one!

Cassidy Rae is a bit like me. She counts the number of Christmas trees in the house windows on the way to work and thrives on the Christmas spirit. But Brad Donovan doesn't share her enthusiasm. Christmas is a painful time of year for him, reminding him of what has slipped out of his grasp. He's just managing to keep his head above water and is looking for a distraction—anything to keep his mind off Christmas. So what happens when the Christmas fairy meets the Grinch? Read on and see.

What I can guarantee you is that there will be snowflakes on Christmas Eve!

Merry Christmas,

Scarlet Wilson

P.S. I love hearing from readers. Come and visit my website, www.scarlet-wilson.com.

# HER CHRISTMAS EVE DIAMOND

## Scarlet Wilson

HARLEQUIN®
entertain, enrich, inspire™

ISBN-13: 978-0-373-06858-6

HER CHRISTMAS EVE DIAMOND

First North American Publication 2012

Check out Scarlet Wilson's fantastic book

WEST WING TO MATERNITY WING!

available in ebook format from www.Harlequin.com.

This book is dedicated to the children I've watched grow up over the years from excitable toddlers into responsible adults: Carissa Hyndman, Jordan Dickson, Dillon Glencross and Carly Glencross. Life is what you make it—reach for the stars!

And to my new editor, Carly Byrne. Thanks for all your support and encouragement. Writing can be a tricky business, and you make it all so much easier—I think we make a good team!

# PROLOGUE

*30 September*

Cassidy raised her hand and knocked on the dilapidated door. Behind her Lucy giggled nervously. 'Are you sure this is the right address?'

Cassidy turned to stare at her. 'You arranged this. How should I know?' She glanced at the crumpled piece of paper in her hand. 'This is definitely number seventeen.' She leaned backwards, looking at the 1960s curtains hanging in the secondary glazed double windows that rattled every time a bus went past. 'Maybe nobody's home?' she said hopefully.

This had to be the worst idea she'd ever had. No. Correction. It hadn't been her idea. In a moment of weakness she'd just agreed to come along with her colleagues to see what all the fuss was about.

'Where did you find this one, Lucy?'

Lucy had spent the past year whisking her friends off to as many different fortune-tellers as possible. By all accounts, some were good, some were bad and some were just downright scary. Cassidy had always managed to wriggle out of it—until now.

'This is the one my cousin Fran came to. She said she was fab.'

Cassidy raised her eyebrows. 'Cousin Fran who went on the reality TV show and then spent the next week hiding in the cupboard?'

Lucy nodded. 'Oh, great,' sighed Cass.

'I wonder if she'll tell me how many children I'll have,' murmured Lynn dreamily. She stuck her pointed elbow into Cassidy's ribs. 'She told Lizzie King she'd have twins and she's due any day now.'

'I just want to know if Frank is ever going to propose,' sighed Tamsin. 'If she doesn't see it in the future then I'm dumping him. Five years is long enough.'

Cassidy screwed up her nose and shook her head. 'You can't dump Frank because of something a fortune-teller says.'

But Tamsin had that expression on her face—the one that said, *Don't mess with me.* 'Watch me.'

There was a shuffle behind the door then

a creak and the door swung open. 'Hello, ladies, come on in.'

Cassidy blinked. The smell of cats hit her
in the face like a steamroller.

She allowed the stampede behind her to
thunder inside then took a deep breath of
clean outside air, before pulling the door
closed behind her. A mangy-looking cat
wound its way around her legs. 'Shoo!' she
hissed.

'Come on, Cassidy!'

She plastered a smile on her face and joined
her colleagues in smelly-cat-woman's front
room. The peeling noise beneath the soles of
her feet told her that the carpet was sticky.
She dreaded to think what with.

Her three friends were crowded onto the
brown sofa. Another cat was crawling across
the back of the sofa behind their heads. Cassidy's eyes started to stream and she resisted
the temptation to start rubbing them. Once
she started, she couldn't stop. Cat allergies
did that to you.

'So who wants to go first?'

Cassidy glanced at her watch. How had she
got roped into this?

'You go first, Cass,' said Lucy, who turned
to smelly-cat woman. 'You'll have to do a

good job, Belinda. Our Cassidy's a non-believer.'

The small, rotund woman eyed Cassidy up and down. Her brow was as wrinkled as her clothes. 'This way, dear,' she muttered, wandering down the hallway to another room.

Cassidy swallowed nervously. Maybe it would be easier to get this over and done with. Then at least she could wait outside in the car for the others.

The room was full of clutter. And cats.

As Belinda settled herself at one side of the table and shuffled some cards, Cassidy eyed the squashed easy chair on the other side. A huge marmalade cat was sitting in pride of place, blinking at her, daring her to move him.

Her gorgeous turquoise-blue velvet pea coat would attract cat hairs like teenage girls to a Bieber concert. She should just kiss it goodbye now.

'Move, Lightning!' Belinda kicked the chair and the cat gave her a hard stare before stretching on his legs and jumping from the seat, settling at her feet.

Cassidy couldn't hide the smile from her face. It had to be the most inappropriately named cat—ever.

Belinda fixed her eyes on her. How could

such a soft, round woman have such a steely glare? Her eyes weren't even blinking. She was staring so hard Cass thought she would bore a hole through her skull.

She looked around her. Books everywhere. Piles of magazines. Shelves and shelves of ornaments, all looking as though they could do with a good dust. Another allergy to set off. One, two, no, three...no, there was another one hiding in the corner. Four cats in the room. All looking at her as if she shouldn't be there. Maybe they knew something that she didn't.

'So, what do we do?' she asked quickly.

Belinda's face had appeared kindly, homely when she'd answered the door. But in here, when it was just the two of them, she looked like a cold and shrewd businesswoman. Cassidy wondered if she could read the thoughts currently in her head. That would account for the light-sabre stare.

Belinda shuffled the cards again. 'We can do whatever you prefer.' She spread the cards face down on the table. 'I can read your cards.' She reached over and grabbed hold of Cassidy's hand. 'I can read your palm. Or...' she glanced around the room '...I can channel some spirits and see what they've got to say.'

The thought sent a chill down Cassidy's

spine. She wasn't sure she believed any of this. But she certainly didn't want to take the risk of channelling any unwanted spirits.

The TV special she'd watched the other day had claimed that all of this was based on reading people. Seeing the tiny, almost imperceptible reactions they had to certain words, certain gestures. Cassidy had come here tonight determined not to move a muscle, not even to blink. But her cat allergy seemed to have got the better of her, and her eyes were a red, blinking, streaming mess. So much for not moving.

She didn't like the look of the cards either. Knowing her luck, she'd turn over the death card—or the equivalent of the Joker.

'Let's just do the palm, please.' It seemed the simplest option. How much could anyone get from some lines on a palm?

Belinda leaned across the table, taking Cassidy's slim hand and wrist and encapsulating them in her pudgy fingers. There was something quite soothing about it. She wasn't examining Cassidy's palm—just holding her hand. Stroking her fingers across the back of her hand for a few silent minutes, then turning her hand over and touching the inside of her palm.

A large smile grew across her face.

The suspense was killing her. Cassidy didn't like long silences. 'What is it?'

Belinda released her hand. 'You're quite the little misery guts, aren't you?'

'What?' Cassidy was stunned. The last she'd heard, these people were only supposed to tell you good things. And certainly not assassinate your character.

Belinda nodded. 'On the surface you're quite the joker with your friends at work. On the other hand, you always see the glass half-empty. Very self-deprecating. All signs of insecurity.' She took a deep breath. 'But very particular at work. Your attention to detail makes you hard to work with. Some of your colleagues just don't know how to take you. And as for men...'

'What?' Right now, men were the last thing on her mind. And the word 'insecurity' had hit a nerve she didn't want to acknowledge. It was bad enough having parents who jet-setted around the world, without having a fiancé who'd upped and left. The last thing she wanted was some random stranger pointing it out to her.

'You're a clever girl, but sometimes you can't see what's right at the end of your nose.' She shook her head. 'You've got some very fixed ideas, and you're not very good at the art of compromise. Just as well Christmas is coming up.'

Cassidy was mad now. 'What's that got to do with anything? Christmas is still three months away.'

Belinda folded her arms across her chest, a smug expression on her face. 'You're going to be a Christmas bride.'

'What?'

The woman had clearly lost her cat-brained mind.

'How on earth can I be a Christmas bride? It's October tomorrow, and I don't have a boyfriend. And there's nobody I'm even remotely interested in.'

Belinda tapped the side of her nose, giving her shoulders an annoying little shrug. 'I only see the future. I don't tell you how you're going to get there.' She leaned over and touched the inside of Cassidy's palm. 'I can see you as a Christmas bride, along with a very handsome groom—not from around these parts either. Lucky you.'

Cassidy shook her head firmly. It had taken her months to get over her broken engagement to her Spanish fiancé—and it had not been an experience she wanted to repeat. 'You're absolutely wrong. There's no way I'm going to be a Christmas bride. And particularly not with a groom from elsewhere. I've had it with foreign men. The next man I hook up with will be a true fellow Scot, through and through.'

Belinda gave her *the look*. The look that said, *You've no idea what you're talking about*.

'That's us, then.'

Cassidy was aghast. Twenty quid for that? 'That's it?'

Belinda nodded and waved her hand. 'Send the next one in.'

Cassidy hesitated for a second, steeling herself to argue with the woman. But then the fat orange cat brushed against her legs and leapt up onto the chair beside her, determined to shed its thousands of orange cat hairs over her velvet coat. She jumped up. At least she was over and done with. She could wait outside in the car. It was almost worth the twenty quid for that alone.

She walked along the corridor, mumbling to herself, attempting to brush a big wad of clumped cat hair from her coat.

'Are you done already? What did she tell you?'

Cassidy rolled her eyes. 'It's not even worth repeating.' She jerked her head down the corridor. 'Go on, Tamsin. Go and find out when you're getting your proposal.'

Tamsin still had that determined look on her face. She stood up and straightened her pristine black mac—no orange cat hairs for her. 'You mean *if* I'm getting my proposal.' She swept down the corridor and banged the door closed behind her.

Lucy raised her eyebrows. 'Heaven help Belinda if she doesn't tell Tam what she wants to hear.' She turned back to Cassidy. 'Come on, then, spill. What did she say?'

Cassidy blew out a long, slow breath through pursed lips. She was annoyed at being called a 'misery guts.' And she was beyond irritated at being called insecure. 'I'm apparently going to be a Christmas bride.'

'*What?*' Lucy's and Lynn's voices were in perfect tandem with their matching shocked expressions.

'Just as well Tamsin didn't hear that,' Lucy muttered.

'Oh, it gets worse. Apparently my groom is from foreign climes.' She rolled her eyes again. 'As if.'

But Lucy's and Lynn's expressions had changed, smiles creeping across their faces as their eyes met.

'Told you.'

'No way.'

Cassidy watched in bewilderment as they high-fived each other in the dingy sitting room.

'What's with you two? You know the whole thing's ridiculous. As if *I'm* going to date another foreign doctor.'

Lynn folded her arms across her chest. 'Stranger things have happened.' She had a weird look on her face. As if she knew something that Cassidy didn't.

Lucy adopted the same pose, shoulder to shoulder with Lynn. Almost as if they were ganging up on her.

Her gaze narrowed. 'I'm willing to place a bet that Belinda could be right.'

Cassidy couldn't believe what was happening. The crazy-cat-woman's disease was obviously contagious. A little seed planted in her brain. She could use this to her advantage. 'What's it worth?'

Lucy frowned. 'What do you mean?'

Cassidy smiled. 'I'll take that bet. But what's it worth?'

'Night shift Christmas Eve. Oh.' The words were out before Lucy had had time to think about them. She had her hand across her mouth. It was the most hated shift on the planet. Every year they had to draw straws to see who would take it.

'You're on.' Cassidy held out her hand towards Lucy, who nodded and shook it firmly. She had no chance of losing this bet. No chance at all.

# CHAPTER ONE

*1 October*

CASSIDY pulled the navy-blue tunic over her head. These new-style NHS uniforms were supposed to be made from a revolutionary lightweight fabric, designed for comfort and ease of fit. The reality was they were freezing and not designed for Scottish winters in a draughty old hospital. She pulled a cardigan from her locker and headed for the stairs. Maybe running up three flights would take the chill out of her bones.

Two minutes later she arrived in the medical ward. She took a deep breath. There it was. The hospital smell. Some people hated it and shuddered walking through the very doors of the hospital. But Cassidy loved it— it was like a big security blanket, and she'd missed it. It was just before seven and the lights were still dimmed. Ruby, the night nurse, gave her a smile. 'Nice to see you back, Cassidy. How was the secondment?'

Cassidy nodded, wrapping her cardigan further around her torso. Her temperature was still barely above freezing. 'It was fine, but three months was long enough. The new community warfarin clinic is set up—all the teething problems ironed out. To be honest, though, I'm glad to be back. I missed this place.'

And she had. But at the time the three-month secondment had been perfect for her. It had given her the chance to sort out all the hassles with her gran, work regular hours and get her settled into the new nursing home— the second in a year. Her eyes swept over the whiteboard on the wall, displaying all the patient names, room numbers and named nurses. 'No beds?' She raised her eyebrows.

'Actually, we've got one. But A and E just phoned to say they're sending us an elderly lady with a chest infection, so I've put her name up on the board already. She should be up in the next ten minutes.'

Cassidy gave a nod as the rest of the day-shift staff appeared, gathering around the nurses' station for the handover report. She waited patiently, listening to the rundown of the thirty patients currently in her general medical ward, before assigning the patients to the nurses on duty and accepting the keys for the medicine and drugs cabinets.

She heard the ominous trundle of a trolley behind her. 'I'll admit this patient,' she told her staff. 'It'll get me back into the swing of things.'

She looked up as Bill, one of the porters, arrived, pulling the trolley with the elderly woman lying on top. A doctor was walking alongside them, carrying some notes and chatting to the elderly lady as they wheeled her into one of the side rooms. He gave her a smile—one that could have launched a thousand toothpaste campaigns. 'This is Mrs Elizabeth Kelly. She's eighty-four and has a history of chronic obstructive pulmonary disease. She's had a chest infection for the last seven days that hasn't responded to oral antibiotics. Her oxygen saturation is down at eighty-two and she's tachycardic. The doctor on call wanted her admitted for IV antibiotics.'

For a moment the strong Australian accent threw her—she hadn't been expecting it. Though goodness knows why not. Her hospital in the middle of Glasgow attracted staff from all over the world. His crumpled blue scrubs and even more crumpled white

coat looked as though he'd slept in them——
and judging by his blond hair, sticking up in
every direction but the right one, he probably had.

She didn't recognise him, which meant
he must be one of the new doctors who had
started while she was away on secondment.
And he was too handsome by far. And that
cheeky twinkle in his eye was already annoying her.

After three months away, some things appeared to have changed around the hospital.
It was usually one of the A and E nurses who
accompanied the patient up to the ward.

Cassidy pumped up the bed and removed
the headboard, pulling the patslide from the
wall and sliding the patient over into the bed.
The doctor helped her put the headboard back
on and adjusted the backrest, rearranging the
pillows so Mrs Kelly could sit upright. Cassidy attached the monitoring equipment and
changed the oxygen supply over to the wall.
The doctor was still standing looking at her.

For a second she almost thought he was
peering at her breasts, but as she followed
his gaze downwards she realised her name
and designation was stitched on the front of
her new tunics.

She held out her hand towards him. 'Cas-

sidy Rae. Sister of the medical receiving unit.
Though from the way you're staring at my
breasts, I take it you've gathered that.'

His warm hand caught her cold one, his
eyes twinkling. 'Pleased to meet you, Dragon
Lady. I hope your heart isn't as cold as your
hands.'

She pulled her hand away from his. 'What
did you call me?'

'Dragon Lady.' He looked unashamed by
the remark. 'Your reputation precedes you.
I've been looking forward to meeting you, although from what I hear it's usually you who
does the name-calling.'

She folded her arms across her chest, trying to stop the edges of her mouth turning
upwards. 'I've no idea what you're talking
about.' She picked up the patient clothing bag
and bent down, starting to unpack Mrs Kelly's belongings into the cabinet next to her
bed.

'I heard you called the last lot Needy,
Greedy and Seedy.'

She jumped. She could feel his warm
breath on her neck. He'd bent forward and
whispered in her ear.

'Who told you that?' she asked incredulously. She glanced at her watch. Ten past
seven on her first morning back, and already

some smart-alec doc was trying to get the better of her.

'Oh, give me a minute.' The mystery doctor ducked out of the room.

It was true. She had nicknamed the last three registrars—all for obvious reasons. One had spent every waking minute eating, the other hadn't seen a patient without someone holding his hand, and as for the last one, he'd spent his year sleazing over all the female staff. And while the nursing staff knew the nicknames she'd given them, she'd no idea who'd told one of the new docs. She'd need to investigate that later.

She stood up and adjusted Mrs Kelly's venturi mask, taking a note of her thin frame and pale, papery skin. Another frail, elderly patient, just like her gran. She altered the alarms on the monitor—at their present setting they would sound every few minutes. With a history of COPD, Mrs Kelly had lower than normal oxygen levels.

'How are you feeling?' She picked up the tympanic thermometer and placed it in Mrs Kelly's ear, pressing the button to read her temperature then recording her observations in the chart. Mrs Kelly shook her pale head.

She sat down at the side of the bed. 'I need to take some details from you, Mrs Kelly.

But how about I get you something to eat and drink first? I imagine you were stuck down in A and E for hours. Would you like some tea? Some toast?'

'Your wish is my command.' The steaming cup of tea and plate of buttered toast thudded down on the bedside table. 'See, Mrs Kelly? I make good on my promises.' He shook his head at Cassidy. 'There was *nothing* to eat down in A and E and I promised I'd get her some tea once we got up here.'

'Thank you, son,' Mrs Kelly said, shifting her mask and lifting the cup to her lips, 'My throat is so dry.'

He nodded slowly. Oxygen therapy frequently made patients' mouths dry and it was important to keep them hydrated.

Cassidy stared at him. Things had changed. She couldn't remember the last time she'd seen a doctor make a patient a cup of tea. It was almost unheard of.

She smiled at him. 'Makes me almost wish we could keep you,' she said quietly. 'You've obviously been well trained.'

His blue eyes glinted. 'And what makes you think you can't keep me?'

'I imagine A and E will have a whole load of patients waiting for you. Why did you come up here anyway? Was it to steal our chocolates?' She nodded towards the nursing station. The medical receiving unit was never short of chocolates, and it wasn't unknown for the doctors from other departments to sneak past and steal some.

He shook his head, the smile still stuck on his face. He held out his hand towards her. 'I forgot to introduce myself earlier. I'm one of yours—though I dread to think what nickname you'll give me. Brad Donovan, medical registrar.'

Cassidy felt herself jerk backwards in surprise. He looked too young to be a medical registrar. Maybe it was the scruffy hair? Or the Australian tan? Or maybe it was that earring glinting in his ear, along with the super-white teeth? He didn't look like any registrar she'd ever met before.

Something twisted inside her gut. No, that wasn't quite true. Bobby. For a tiny second he reminded her of Bobby. But Bobby's hair had been dark, not blond, and he'd worn it in a similar scruffy style and had the same glistening white teeth. She pushed all thoughts away. She hadn't thought about him in months. Where had that come from?

She focused her mind. This was a work colleague—albeit a cheeky one. She shook his hand firmly. 'Well, Dr Donovan, if you're one of mine then maybe I should tell you the rules in my ward.'

His eyebrows rose, an amused expression on his face. 'You really are the Dragon Lady, aren't you?'

She ignored him. 'When you finally manage to put some clothes on, no silly ties. In fact, no ties at all and no long sleeves. They're an infection-control hazard.' She ran her eyes up and down his crumpled scrubs, 'Though from the look of you, that doesn't seem to be a problem. Always use the gel outside the patients' rooms before you touch them. And pay attention to what my nurses tell you— they spend most of their day with the patients and will generally know the patients ten times better than you will.'

His blue eyes fixed on hers. Quite unnerving for this time in the morning. His gaze was straight and didn't falter. The guy was completely unfazed by her. He seemed confident, self-assured. She would have to wait and see if his clinical competence matched his demeanour.

'I have been working here for the last two months without your rulebook. I'm sure your staff will give me a good report.' She resisted the temptation to reply. Of course her staff would give him a good report. He was like a poster boy for Surfers' Central. She could put money on it that he'd spent the last two months charming her staff with his lazy accent, straight white teeth and twinkling eyes. He handed her Mrs Kelly's case notes and prescription chart.

'I've written Mrs Kelly up for some IV antibiotics, some oral steroids and some bronchodilators. She had her arterial blood gases done in A and E and I'll check them again in a few hours. I'd like her on four-hourly obs in the meantime.' He glanced at the oxygen supply, currently running at four litres. 'Make sure she stays on the twenty-eight per cent venturi mask. One of the students in A and E didn't understand the complications of COPD and put her on ten litres of straight oxygen.'

Cassidy's mouth fell open. 'Please tell me you're joking.'

He shook his head. The effects could have been devastating. 'Her intentions were good. Mrs Kelly's lips were blue from lack of oxygen when she was admitted. The student just did what seemed natural. Luckily one of the other staff spotted her mistake quickly.'

Cassidy looked over at the frail, elderly lady on the bed, her oxygen mask currently dangling around her neck as she munched the toast from the plate in front of her. The blue tinge had obviously disappeared from her lips, but even eating the toast was adding to her breathlessness. She turned back to face Brad. 'Any relatives?'

He shook his head. 'Her husband died a few years ago and her daughter emigrated to my neck of the woods ten years before that.' He pointed to a phone number in the records. 'Do you want me to phone her, or do you want to do that?'

Cassidy felt a little pang. This poor woman must be lonely. She'd lost her husband, and her daughter lived thousands of miles away. Who did she speak to every day? One of the last elderly patients admitted to her ward had disclosed that often he went for days without a single person to speak to. Loneliness could be a terrible burden.

The doctor passed in front of her vision again, trying to catch her attention, and she pushed the uncomfortable thoughts from her head. This one was definitely too good to be true. Bringing up a patient, making tea and toast, and offering to phone relatives?

Her internal radar started to ping. She turned to Mrs Kelly. 'I'll let you finish your tea and come back in a few minutes.

'What are you up to?' She headed out the door towards the nursing station.

He fell into step beside her. 'What do you mean?'

She paused in the corridor, looking him up and down. 'You're too good to be true. Which means alarm bells are ringing in my head. What's with the nice-boy act?'

She pulled up the laptop from the nurses' station and started to input some of Mrs Kelly's details.

'Who says it's an act?'

Her eyes swept down the corridor. The case-note trolley had been pulled to the end of the corridor. Two other doctors in white coats were standing, talking over some notes. She looked at her watch—not even eight o'clock. 'And who are they?'

Brad smiled. 'That's the other registrars. Luca is from Italy, and Franco is from Hungary. They must have wanted to get a head start on the ward round.' He gave her a brazen wink. 'I guess they heard the Dragon Lady was on duty today.'

She shook her head in bewilderment. 'I go on secondment for three months, come back and I've got the poster boy for Surfers' Paradise making tea and toast for patients and two other registrars in the ward before eight a.m. Am I still dreaming? Have I woken up yet?'

'Why?' As quick as a flash he'd moved

around beside her. 'Am I the kind of guy you dream about?'

'Get lost, flyboy.' She pushed Mrs Kelly's case notes back into his hands. 'You've got a patient's daughter in Australia to go and phone. Make yourself useful while I go and find out what kind of support system she has at home.'

He paused for a second, his eyes narrowing. 'She's not even heated up the bed yet and you're planning on throwing her back out?'

Cassidy frowned. 'It's the basic principle of the receiving unit. Our first duty is to find out what systems are in place for our patients. Believe it or not, most of them don't like staying here. And if we plan ahead it means there's less chance of a delayed discharge. Sometimes it can take a few days to set up support systems to get someone home again.' She raised her hand to the whiteboard with patient names. 'In theory, we're planning for their discharge as soon as they enter A and E.'

The look on his face softened. 'In that case, I'll let you off.' He nodded towards his fellow doctors. 'Maybe they got the same alarm call that I did. Beware the Dragon!' He headed towards the doctors' office to make his call.

* * *

Dragon Lady was much more interesting than he'd been led to believe. He'd expected a sixty-year-old, grey-haired schoolmarm. Instead he'd got a young woman with a slim, curvy figure, chestnut curls and deep brown eyes. And she was feisty. He liked that.

Cassidy Rae could be fun. There it was, that strange, almost unfamiliar feeling. That first glimmer of interest in a woman. That tiny little thought that something could spark between them given half a chance. It had been so long since he'd felt it that he almost didn't know what to do about it.

He'd been here a few months, and while his colleagues were friendly, they weren't his 'friends'. And he didn't want to hang around with the female junior doctors currently batting their eyelids at him. Experience had taught him it was more trouble than it was worth.

*Distraction.* The word echoed around his head again as he leaned against the cold concrete wall.

Exactly what he needed. Something to keep his mind from other things—like another Christmas Day currently looming on the horizon with a huge black stormcloud hovering over it. He'd even tried to juggle the schedules so he could be working on Christmas

Day. But no such luck. His Italian colleague had beat him to it, and right now he couldn't bear the thought of an empty Christmas Day in strange surroundings with no real friends or family.

Another Christmas spent wondering where his little girl was, if she was enjoying her joint birthday and Christmas Day celebrations. Wondering if she even remembered he existed.

He had no idea what she'd been told about him. The fact he'd spent the last eighteen months trying to track down his daughter at great time and expense killed him—especially in the run-up to her birthday. Everyone else around him was always full of festive spirit and fun, and no matter how hard he tried not to be the local misery guts, something inside him just felt dead.

Christmas was about families and children. And the one thing he wanted to do was sit his little girl on his knee and get her the biggest birthday and Christmas present in the world. If only he knew where she was...

There was that fist again, hovering around his stomach, tightly clenched. Every time he thought of his daughter, Melody, the visions of her mother, Alison, a junior doctor he'd worked with, appeared in his head. Alison, the woman who only liked things her way or no way at all. No negotiation. No compromise.

More importantly, no communication.

The woman who'd left a bitter taste in his mouth for the last eighteen months. Blighting every other relationship he'd tried to have. The woman who'd wrangled over every custody arrangement, telling him he was impinging on her life. Then one day that had been it. Nothing. He'd gone to pick up two-year-old Melody as planned and had turned up at an empty house. No forwarding address. Nothing.

The colleagues at the hospital where Alison had worked said she'd thought about going to America—apparently she'd fallen head over heels in love with some American doctor. But no one knew where. And he'd spent the last few years getting his solicitor to chase false leads halfway around the world. It had taken over his whole world. Every second of every day had revolved around finding his daughter. Until he'd finally cracked and some good friends had sat him down firmly and spoken to him.

It had only been in the last few months, since moving to Scotland, that he'd finally started to feel like himself again. His laid-back manner had returned, and he'd finally started to relax and be comfortable in his own skin again.

While he would still do everything in his power to find his daughter, he had to realise his limitations. He had to accept the fact he hadn't done anything wrong and he still deserved to live a life.

And while the gaggle of nurses and female junior doctors didn't appeal to him, Cassidy Rae did. She was a different kettle of fish altogether. A fierce, sassy woman who could help him make some sparks fly. A smile crept over his face. Now there was just the small matter of the duty room to break to her. How would she react to that?

Cassidy went back to Mrs Kelly and finished her admission paperwork, rechecked her obs and helped her wash and change into a clean nightdress. By the time she'd finished, Mrs Kelly was clearly out of breath again. Even the slightest exertion seemed to fatigue her.

Cassidy hung the IV antibiotics from the drip stand and connected up the IV. 'These will take half an hour to go through. The doctor has changed the type of antibiotic that you're on so hopefully they'll be more effective than the ones you were taking at home.'

Mrs Kelly nodded. 'Thanks, love. He's a nice one, isn't he?' There was a little pause. 'And he's single. Told me so himself.'

'Who?' Cassidy had started to tidy up around about her, putting away the toilet bag and basin.

'That handsome young doctor. Reminds of that guy on TV. You know, the one from the soap opera.'

Cassidy shook her head. 'I don't watch soap operas. And anyway...' she bundled up the used towels and sheets to put in the laundry trolley '...I'm looking for a handsome Scotsman. Not someone from the other side of the world.'

She walked over to the window. The old hospital building was several storeys high, on the edge of the city. The grey clouds were hanging low this morning and some drizzly rain was falling outside, but she could still see some greenery in the distance.

'Why on earth would anyone want to leave all this behind?' she joked.

Mrs Kelly raised her eyebrows. 'Why indeed?'

Cassidy spent the rest of the morning finding her feet again in the ward. The hospital computer system had been updated, causing her to lose half her patients at the touch of a button. And the automated pharmacy delivery seemed to be on the blink again. Some poor patients' medicines would be lost in a pod stuck in a tube somewhere.

Lucy appeared from the ward next door, clutching a cup of tea, and tapped her on the shoulder. 'How does it feel to be back?'

Cassidy gave her friend a smile. 'It's good.' She picked up the off-duty book. 'I just need to get my head around the rosters again.' Her eyes fell on the sticky notes inside the book and she rolled her eyes. 'Oh, great. Seven members of staff want the same weekend off.'

Lucy laughed. 'That's nothing. One of our girls got married last weekend and I had to rope in two staff from the next ward to cover the night shift. Got time for a tea break?'

She shook her head and pointed down the corridor. 'The consultant's just about to arrive for the ward round.'

Lucy crossed her arms across her chest as she followed Cassidy's gaze to the three registrars at the bottom of the corridor. 'So what do you make of our new docs?'

Cassidy never even lifted her head. 'Funky, Chunky and Hunky?'

Lucy spluttered tea all down the front of her uniform. She looked at her watch. 'Less than two hours and you've got nicknames for them already?'

Cassidy lifted her eyebrows. 'It wasn't hard. Although Luca is drop-dead gorgeous, he's more interested in his own reflection than any of the patients. And Franco has finished off two rolls with sausages and half a box of chocolates in the last half hour.'

'So none of them have caught your eye, then?'

Cassidy turned her head at the tone in her friend's voice. She looked at her suspiciously. 'Why? What are you up to?'

Lucy's gaze was still fixed down the corridor. 'Nothing. I just wondered what you thought of them.' She started to shake her behind as she wiggled past, singing along about single ladies.

Cassidy looked back down the corridor. Her eyes were drawn in one direction. Brad's appearance hadn't improved. He was still wearing his crumpled scrubs and coat. His hair was still untamed and she could see a shadow around his jaw.

But he had spent nearly half an hour talking to Mrs Kelly's daughter and then another half hour talking Mrs Kelly through her treatment for the next few days. Then trying to persuade her that once she was fit and well, she might want to take up her daughter's offer of a visit to Australia.

Most doctors she worked with weren't that interested in their patients' holistic care. Their radar seemed to switch off as soon as they'd made a clinical diagnosis.

There was the sound of raucous laughter at the end of the corridor, and Cassidy looked up to see Brad almost bent double, talking to one of the male physios.

She shook her head and scoured the ward, looking for one of the student nurses. 'Karen?'

The student scuttled over. 'Yes, Sister?'

'Do you know how to assess a patient for the risk of pressure ulcers?'

The student nodded quickly as Cassidy handed her a plastic card with the Waterlow scale on it. 'I want you to do Mrs Kelly's assessment then come back and we'll go over it together.'

Karen nodded and hurried off down the corridor. Cassidy watched for a second. With her paper-thin skin, poor nutrition and lack of circulating oxygen, Mrs Kelly was at real risk of developing pressure sores on her body. For Cassidy, the teaching element was one of the reasons she did this job. She wanted all the students who came through her ward to understand the importance of considering all aspects of their patients' care.

There was a thud beside her. Brad was in the chair next to her, his head leaning on one hand, staring at her again with those blue eyes. He couldn't wipe the smile from his face. 'So, which one am I?'

Cassidy blew a wayward chestnut curl out of her face. 'What are you talking about now?'

He moved closer. 'Hunky, Chunky or Funky? Which one am I?' He put his hands together and pleaded in front of her. 'Please tell me I'm Hunky.'

'How on earth did you…?' Her eyes looked down the corridor to where Pete, the physio, was in conversation with one of the other doctors. He must have overheard her. 'Oh, forget it.'

She wrinkled her nose at him, leaning forward wickedly so nobody could hear. 'No way are you Hunky. That's reserved for the Italian god named Luca.' Her eyes fell on Luca, standing talking to one of her nurses. She whispered in Brad's ear, 'Have you noticed how he keeps checking out his own reflection in those highly polished Italian shoes of his?'

Brad's shoulders started to shake.

She prodded him on the shoulder. 'No.

With that excuse of a haircut and that strange earring, you're definitely Funky.' She pointed at his ear. 'What is that anyway?'

Her head came forward, her nose just a few inches off his ear as she studied the twisted bit of gold in his ear. 'Is it a squashed kangaroo? Or a surfboard?'

'Neither.' He grinned at her, turning his head so their noses nearly touched. 'Believe it or not, it used to be a boomerang. My mum bought it for me when I was a teenager and I won a competition.' He touched it with his finger. 'It's a little bent out of shape now.'

Her face was serious and he could smell her perfume— or her shampoo. She smelled of strawberries. A summer smell, even though it was the middle of winter in Glasgow. He was almost tempted to reach out and touch her chestnut curls, resting just above her collarbone. But she was staring at him with those big chocolate-brown eyes. And he didn't want to move.

If this was the Dragon Lady of the medical receiving unit, he wondered if he could be her St George and try to tame her. No. That was the English patron saint and he was in Scotland. He'd learned quickly not to muddle things up around here. The Scots he'd met were wildly patriotic.

Her face broke into a smile again. Interesting. She hadn't pulled back, even though they were just inches from each other. She didn't seem intimidated by his closeness. In any other circumstances he could have leaned forward and given her a kiss. A perfect example of the sort of distraction he needed.

'Come to think of it, though...' She glanced up and down his crumpled clothes. How could she ever have thought he reminded her of Bobby? Bobby wouldn't have been seen dead in crumpled clothes. He'd always been immaculate—Brad was an entirely different kettle of fish. 'If you keep coming into my ward dressed like that, I'll have to change your name from Funky to Skunky.'

Brad automatically sat backwards in his chair, lowering his chin and sniffing. 'Why, do I smell? I was on call last night and I haven't been in the shower yet.' He started to pull at his scrub top.

She loved it. The expression of worry on his face. The way she could so easily wind him up. And the fact he had a good demeanour with the patients and staff. This guy might even be a little fun to have around. Even if he was from the other side of the world.

She shook her head. 'Stop panicking, Brad. You don't smell.' She rested her head on her hands for a second, fixing him with her eyes. Mornings on the medical receiving unit were always chaotic. Patients to be moved to other wards, new admissions and usually a huge battery of tests to be arranged. Sometimes it was nice just to take a few seconds of calm, before chaos erupted all around you.

He reached over and touched her hand, resting on top of the off-duty book. The invisible electric jolt that shot up her arm was instantaneous.

'I could help you with those. The last place I worked in Australia had a computer system for duty rosters. You just put in the names, your shift patterns and the requests. It worked like a charm.'

Her eyes hadn't left where his hand was still touching hers. It was definitely lingering there. She'd just met this guy.

'You're going to be a pest, aren't you?' Her voice was low. For some reason she couldn't stop staring at him. It didn't help that he was easy on the eye. And that scraggy hair was kind of growing on her.

He leaned forward again. 'Is that going to be a problem?' His eyes were saying a thousand different words from his mouth. Something was in the air between them. She could practically feel the air around her crackle.

This was ridiculous. She felt like a swooning teenager.

'My gran had a name for people like you.'

He moved even closer. 'And what was that?' He tilted his head to one side. 'Handsome? Clever? Smart?'

She shook her head and stood up, straightening her tunic. 'Oh, no. It was much more fitting. My gran would have called you a "wee scunner".'

His brow wrinkled. 'What on earth does that mean?'

'Just like I told you. A nuisance. A pest. But it's a much more accurate description.' She headed towards the duty room, with the off-duty book in her hand. She had to get away from him. Her brain had taken leave of her senses. She should have taken Lucy up on that offer of tea.

Brad caught her elbow. 'Actually, Cassidy, about your duty room…'

He stopped as she pushed the door open and automatically stepped inside, her foot catching on something.

'Wh-h-a-a-t?'

# CHAPTER TWO

CASSIDY stared up at the white ceiling of her duty room, the wind knocked clean out of her. Something was sticking into her ribcage and she squirmed, causing an array of perilously perched cardboard boxes to topple over her head. She squealed again, batting her hands in front of her face.

A strong pair of arms grabbed her wrists and yanked her upwards, standing her on the only visible bit of carpet in the room—right at the doorway.

Brad was squirming. 'Sorry about that, Cassidy. I was trying to warn you but…'

He stopped in mid-sentence. She looked mad. She looked *really* mad. Her chestnut curls were in complete disarray, falling over her face and hiding her angry eyes. 'What is all this rubbish?' she snapped.

Brad cleared his throat. 'Well, actually, it's not "rubbish", as you put it. It's mine.' He bent over and started pushing some files back into an overturned box. They were the last thing he wanted anyone to see.

Her face was growing redder by the second. She looked down at her empty hand—obviously wondering where the off-duty book she'd been holding had got to. She bent forward to look among the upturned boxes then straightened up, shaking her head in disgust.

She planted her hands on her hips. 'You'd better have a good explanation for this. No wonder you were giving me the treatment.'

'What treatment?'

She waved her hand in dismissal. 'You know. The smiles. The whispers. The big blue eyes.' She looked at him mockingly. 'You must take me for a right sap.'

All of a sudden Brad understood the Dragon Lady label. When she was mad, she was *mad*. Heaven help the doctor who messed up on her watch.

He leaned against the doorjamb. 'I wasn't giving you the *treatment*, as you put it, Cassidy. I was trying to connect with the sister of the ward I work in. We're going to have to work closely together, and I'd like it if we were friends.'

Her face softened ever so slightly. She

looked at the towering piles of boxes obliterating her duty room. 'And all this?'

He shot her a smile. 'Yes, well, there's a story about all that.'

She ran her fingers through her hair, obviously attempting to re-tame it. He almost wished he could do it for her. 'Please don't tell me you've moved in.'

He laughed. 'No. It's not that desperate. I got caught short last night and was flung out of my flat, so I had to bring all my stuff here rather than leave it all sitting in the street.'

She narrowed her eyes. 'What do you mean, you got caught short? That sounds suspiciously like you were having a party at five in the morning and the landlord threw you out.'

Brad nodded slowly. 'Let's just say I broke one of the rules of my tenancy.'

'Which one?'

'Now, that would be telling.' He pulled a set of keys from his pocket with a brown tag attached. 'But help is at hand. I've got a new flat I can move into tonight—if I can find it.'

'What do you mean—if you can find it?' Cassidy bent over and read the squiggly writing on the tag.

Brad shrugged his shoulders. 'Dowangate Lane. I'm not entirely sure where it is. One of the porters put me onto it at short notice. I needed somewhere that was furnished and was available at short notice. He says its only five minutes away from here, but I don't recognise the street name.'

Cassidy gave him a suspicious look. 'I don't suppose anyone told you that I live near there.'

'Really? No, I'd no idea. Can you give me some directions?'

Cassidy sighed. 'Sure. Go out the front of the hospital, take a left, walk a few hundred yards down the road, take a right, go halfway down the street and go down the nearby close. Dowangate Lane runs diagonally off it. But the street name fell off years ago.'

Cassidy had a far-away look in her eyes and was gesturing with her arms. Her voice got quicker and quicker as she spoke, her Scottish accent getting thicker by the second.

'I have no idea what you just said.'

Cassidy stared at him—hard. 'It would probably be easier if I just showed you.'

'Really? Would you?'

'If it means you'll get all this rubbish out of my duty room, it will be worth it.'

'Gee, thanks.'

'Do you want my help or not?'

He bent forward and caught her gesturing

arms. 'I would love your help, Cassidy Rae.
How does six o'clock sound?' There it was
again—that strawberry scent from her hair.
That could become addictive.

She stopped talking. He could feel the little goose-bumps on her bare arms. Was she
cold? Or was it something else?

Whatever it was, he was feeling it, too. Not
some wild, throw-her-against-the-wall attraction, although he wouldn't mind doing that. It
was weird. Some kind of connection.

Maybe he wasn't the only person looking
for a Christmastime distraction.

She was staring at him with those big
brown eyes again. Only a few seconds must
have passed but it felt like minutes.

He could almost hear her thought pro-
cesses. As if she was wondering what was
happening between them, too.

'Six o'clock will be fine,' she said finally,
as she lowered her eyes and brushed past him.

Brad hung his white coat up behind the door
and pulled his shirt over his head. He paused
midway. What was he going to do with it?

Cass stuck her head around the door.
'Are you ready yet?' Her eyes caught the
tanned, taut abdomen and the words stuck
in her throat. She felt the colour rush into her

cheeks. 'Oops, sorry.' She pulled back from the door.

All of a sudden she felt like a teenager again. And trust him to have a set of to-die-for abs. Typical. There was no way she was ever taking her clothes off in front of Mr Ripped Body.

*Where had that come from?* Why on earth would she ever take her clothes off in front of him? That was it. She was clearly losing her marbles.

Almost automatically, she sucked in her stomach and looked downwards. Her pink jumper hid a multitude of sins, so why on earth was she bothering?

Brad's hand rested on the edge of the door as he stuck his head back round. 'Don't be so silly, Cassidy. You're a nurse. It's not like you haven't seen it all before. Come back in. I'll be ready in a second.'

She swallowed the huge lump at the back of her throat. His shoulder was still bare. He was obviously used to stripping off in front of women and was completely uninhibited.

So why did that thought rankle her?

She took a deep breath and stepped back into the room, trying to avert her eyes without being obvious. The last thing she wanted was for him to think she was embarrassed. With an attitude like his, she'd never live it down.

He was rummaging in a black holdall. Now she could see the muscles across his back. No love handles for him. He yanked a pale blue T-shirt from the bag and pulled it over his head, turning round and tugging it down over his washboard stomach.

'Ready. Can we go?'

Cassidy had a strange expression on her face. Brad automatically looked down. Did he have a huge ketchup stain on his T-shirt? Not that he could see. Her cheeks were slightly flushed, matching the soft pink jumper she was wearing. A jumper that hugged the shape of her breasts very nicely. Pink was a good colour on her. It brought out the warm tones in her face and hair that had sometimes been lost in the navy-blue tunic she'd been wearing earlier. Her hair was pulled back from her face in a short ponytail, with a few wayward curls escaping. She was obviously serious about helping him move. No fancy coats and stiletto heels for her. Which was just as well as there were around fifty boxes to lug over to his new flat.

'Will you manage to carry some of these boxes down to my car?'

'I'll do better than that.' She opened the

door to reveal one of the porters' trolleys for transporting boxes of equipment around the hospital. The huge metal cage could probably take half of his boxes in one run.

'Genius. You might be even more useful than I thought.'

'See, I'm not just a pretty face,' she shot back, to his cheeky remark. 'You do realise this is going to cost you, don't you?' She pulled the cage towards the duty room, letting him stand in the doorway and toss out boxes that she piled up methodically.

'How much?' As he tossed one of the boxes, the cardboard flaps sprang open, spilling his boxers and socks all over the floor.

Cassidy couldn't resist. The colours of every imagination caught her eyes and she lifted up a pair with Elmo from *Sesame Street* emblazoned on the front. 'Yours?' she asked, allowing them to dangle from one finger.

He grabbed them. 'Stop it.' He started ramming them back into the box, before raising his eyebrows at her. 'I'll decide when you get to see my underwear.'

*When. Not if.* The thought catapulted through her brain as she tried to keep her mind on the job at hand. The boxes weren't neatly packed or taped shut. And the way he kept throwing them at her was ruining her precision stacking in the metal cage.

'Slow down,' she muttered. 'The more you irritate me, the more my price goes up. You're currently hovering around a large pizza or a sweet-and-sour chicken. Keep going like this and you'll owe me a beer as well.'

The cheeky grin appeared at her shoulder in an instant. 'You think I won't buy you a beer?' He stared at the neatly stacked boxes. 'Uh-oh. I sense a little obsessive behaviour. One of your staff warned me about wrecking the neatly packed boxes of gloves in the treatment room. I can see why.'

'Nothing wrong with being neat and tidy.' Cassidy straightened the last box. 'Okay, I think that's enough for now. We can take the rest downstairs on the second trip.'

Something flashed in front of his eyes. Something wicked. 'You think so?'

He waited while she nodded, then as quick as a flash he shoved her in the cage, clicking the door behind her and pushing the cage down the corridor.

Cassidy let out a squeal. For the second time today she was surrounded by piles of toppling boxes. 'Let me out!' She got to her knees in the cage as he stopped in front of the lifts and pushed the 'down' button.

His shoulders were shaking with laughter as he pulled a key from his pocket for the 'Supplies Only' lift and opened the door. 'What can I say? You bring out the wicked side in me. I couldn't resist wrecking your neat display.'

He pulled the cage into the lift and sprang the lock free, holding out his hands to steady her step. The lift started with a judder, and as she was in midstep—it sent her straight into his arms. 'Ow-w!

The lift was small. Even smaller with the large storage cage and two people crammed inside. And as Brad had pressed the ground-floor button as he'd pulled the cage inside, they were now trapped at the back of the lift together.

She was pressed against him. He could feel the ample swell of her breasts against his chest, her soft pink jumper tickling his skin. His hands had fallen naturally to her waist, one finger touching a little bit of soft flesh. Had she noticed?

Her curls were under his nose, but there was no way he was moving his hands to scratch the itch. She lifted her head, capturing him with her big brown eyes again.

*This was crazy. This was madness.*

This was someone he'd just met today. It

didn't matter that he felt a pull towards her. It didn't matter that she'd offered to help him. It didn't matter that for some strange reason he liked to be close to her. It didn't matter that his eyes were currently fixed on her plump lips. He knew nothing about her.

Her reputation had preceded her. According to her colleagues she was a great nurse and a huge advocate for her patients, but her attention to detail and rulebook for the ward had become notorious.

More importantly, she knew nothing about him. She had no idea about his history, his family, his little girl out there in the world somewhere. She had no idea how the whole thing had come close to breaking him. And for some reason he didn't want to tell her.

He wanted this to be separate. A flirtation. A distraction. Something playful. With no consequences. Even if it only lasted a few weeks.

At least that would get him past Christmas.

'You can let me go now.' Her voice was quiet, her hands resting on his upper arms sending warm waves through his bare skin.

But for a second they just stood there. Unmoving.

The door pinged open and they turned their heads. His hands fell from her waist.

She turned and automatically pushed the cage through the lift doors, and he fell into step next to her.

The tone and mood were broken.

'Are you sure you don't mind helping me with this? You could always just draw me a map.'

She stuck her elbow in his ribs. 'Stop trying to get out of buying me dinner. What number did you say the flat was? If I find out I've got to carry all these boxes up four flights of stairs I *won't* be happy.'

They crossed the car park and reached his car. She blinked. A Mini. For a guy that was over six feet tall.

'This is your car?'

'Do you like it?' He opened the front passenger door, moved the seat forward and started throwing boxes in the back. 'It's bigger than you think.'

'Why on earth didn't you just leave some stuff in the car?'

Brad shrugged. 'Luca borrowed my car last night after he helped me move my stuff. I think he had a date.' And some of his boxes were far too personal to be left unguarded in a car.

Cassidy shook her head and opened the boot, trying to cram as many of the boxes in there as possible. She was left with two of the larger ones still sitting on the ground.

She watched as he put the passenger seat back into place and shrugged her shoulders. 'I can just put these two on my lap. It's only a five-minute drive. It'll be fine.'

Brad pulled a face. 'You might need to put something else on your lap instead.'

She felt her stomach turn over. What now?

'Why do I get the distinct impression that nothing is straightforward with you?'

He grabbed her hand and pulled her towards the porter's lodge at the hospital gate, leaving the two boxes next to his unlocked car. 'Come on.'

'Where on earth are we going?'

'I've got something else to pick up.'

He pushed open the door to the lodge. Usually used for deliveries and collections, occasionally used by the porters who were trying to duck out of sight for five minutes, it was an old-fashioned solid stone building. The front door squeaked loudly. 'Frank? Are you there?'

Frank Wallace appeared. All twenty-five stone of him, carrying a pile of white-and-black fur in his hands. 'There you are, Dr Donovan. He's been as good as gold. Not a bit of bother. Bring him back any time.'

Frank handed over the bundle of black and white, and it took a few seconds for Cassidy to realise the shaggy bundle was a dog with a bright red collar and lead.

Brad bent down and placed the dog on the floor at their feet. It seemed to spring to life, the head coming up sharply and a little tail wagging furiously. Bright black eyes and a pink panting tongue.

'Cassidy, meet Bert. *This* is the reason I lost my tenancy.'

Cassidy watched in amazement. Bert seemed delighted to see him, jumping his paws up onto Brad's shoulders and licking at his hands furiously. His gruff little barks reverberated around the stone cottage.

He was a scruffy little mutt—with no obvious lineage or pedigree. A mongrel, by the look of him.

'Why on earth would you have a dog?' she asked incredulously. 'You live in Australia. You can't possibly have brought him with you.' Dogs she could deal with. It was cats that caused her allergies. She'd often thought about getting a pet for company—a friendly face to come home to. But long shifts weren't conducive to having a pet. She knelt on the floor next to Brad, holding her hand out cautiously while Bert took a few seconds to sniff her, before licking her with the same enthusiasm he'd shown Brad.

'I found him. A few weeks ago, in the street outside my flat. He looked emaciated and was crouched in a doorway. There was no way I could leave him alone.' *And to be honest, I needed him as much as he needed me.* Brad let the scruffy dog lick his hands. Melody would love this little dog.

'So what did you do?'

'I took him to the emergency vet, who checked him over, gave me some instructions, then I took him home.'

'And *this* is why you got flung out your flat?' There was an instant feeling of relief. He hadn't been thrown out for non-payment of rent, wild parties or dubious women. He'd been thrown out because of a dog. She glanced at his face as he continued to talk to Bert. The mutual admiration was obvious.

The rat. He must have known that a dog would have scored him brownie points. No wonder he'd kept it quiet earlier. She would have taken him for a soft touch.

She started to laugh. 'Bert? You called your dog Bert?'

He shrugged his shoulders. 'What's wrong with Bert? It's a perfectly good name.'

'What's wrong with Rocky or Buster or Duke?'

He waved his hand at her. 'Look at him. Does he look like Rocky, Buster or Duke?'

He waited a few seconds, and Bert obligingly tipped his head to one side, as if he enjoyed the admiration.

Brad was decisive. 'No way. He's a Bert. No doubt about it.'

Cassidy couldn't stop the laugh that had built up in her chest. Bert wasn't a big dog and his white hair with black patches had definitely seen better days. But his soft eyes and panting tongue were cute. And Brad was right. He looked like a Bert—it suited him. She bent down and started rubbing his ears.

'See—you like him. Everyone should. He's a good dog. Not been a bit of bother since I found him.'

'So how come you got flung out the flat? And what about the new one? I take it they're happy for you to have a dog?'

Brad pulled a face. 'One of my neighbours reported me for having a dog. And the landlord was swift and ruthless, even though you honestly wouldn't have known he was there. And it was Frank, the porter, who put me onto the new flat. So I'm sorted. They're happy for me to have a dog.'

Cassidy held out her arms to pick up the dog. 'I take it this is what I'm supposed to have on my lap in the car?'

Brad nodded. 'Thank goodness you like dogs. This could have all turned ugly.'

She shook her head, still rubbing Bert's ears. 'I'm sure it will be fine. But let's go. It's getting late and I'm starving.'

They headed back to the car and drove down the road past Glasgow University and into the west end of Glasgow. Lots of the younger hospital staff stayed in the flats around here. It wasn't really designed for kids and families, but for younger folks it was perfect, with the shops, restaurants and nightlife right at their fingertips.

'So what do you like best about staying around here?'

Cassidy glanced around about her as they drove along Byres Road. She pointed to the top of the road. 'If you go up there onto Western Road and cross the road, you get to Glasgow's Botanic Gardens. Peace, perfect peace.'

Brad looked at her in surprise. 'Really? That's a bit unusual for someone your age.'

'Why would you think that? Is it only pensioners and kids that can visit?' She gestured her thumb over her shoulder. 'Or if you go back that way, my other favourite is the Kelvingrove Art Gallery and Museum—as long as the school trips aren't there! There's even a little secret church just around the corner with an ancient cemetery—perfect for quiet book reading in the summer. Gorgeous at Christmastime.'

Brad stared at her. 'You're a dark horse, aren't you? I never figured you for a museum type.'

She shrugged her shoulders. 'It's the peace and quiet really. The ward can be pretty hectic. Some days when I come out I'm just looking for somewhere to chill. I can be just as happy curled up with a good book or in the dark at the cinema.'

'You go to the cinema alone?'

She nodded. 'All the time. I love sci-fi. My friends all love romcoms. So I do some with my friends and some on my own.' She pointed her arm in front of them. 'Turn left here, then turn right and slow down.'

The car pulled to a halt at the side of the road next to some bollards. Cassidy looked downwards. Bert had fallen asleep in her lap. 'Looks like it's been a big day for the little guy.'

Brad jumped out of and around the car and opened the passenger door. He picked up the sleeping dog. 'Let's go up and have a look at the flat before I start to unpack the boxes.'

'You haven't seen it yet?'

He shook his head. 'How could I? I was on call last night and just had to take whatever I could get. I told you I'd no idea where this place was.'

Cassidy smiled. 'So you did. Silly me. Now, give me the key and we'll see what you've got.'

They climbed up the stairs in the old-style tenement building, onto the first floor, where number five was in front of them. Cassidy looked around. 'Well, this is better than some flats I've seen around here.' She ran her hand along the wall. 'The walls have been painted, the floors are clean, and…' she pointed to the door across the hallway '…your neighbour has some plants outside his flat. This place must be okay.'

She turned the key in the lock and pushed open the door. Silently praying that she wouldn't be hit with the smell of cats, mould or dead bodies.

Brad flicked the light switch next to the door and stepped inside. He was trying to stop his gut from twisting. Getting a flat that accepted dogs at short notice—and five minutes away from the hospital—seemed almost too good to be true. There had to be a catch somewhere.

The catch was obvious. Cassidy burst into fits of laughter.

'No way! It's like stepping back in time. Have we just transported into the 1960s?' She turned to face him. 'That happened once in an old *Star Trek* episode. I think we're just reliving it.'

Brad was frozen. The wallpaper could set off a whole array of seizures. He couldn't even make out the individual colours, the purples and oranges all seemed to merge into one. As for the shag-pile brown carpet...

Cassidy was having the time of her life. She dashed through one of the open doors and let out a shriek. 'Avacado! It's avocado. You have an avocado bathroom! Does that colour even exist any more?' Seconds later he heard the sounds of running water before she appeared again, tears flowing down her cheeks. 'I love this place. You have to have a 1960s-style party.'

She ducked into another room then swept past him into the kitchen, while Brad tried to keep his breathing under control. Could he really live in this?

He set down the dog basket on the floor and placed the sleeping Bert inside. His quiet, peaceful dog would probably turn into a possessed, rabid monster in this place.

He sagged down onto the purple sofa that clashed hideously with the brown shag-pile carpet. No wonder this place had been available at a moment's notice.

He could hear banging and clattering from next door—Cassidy had obviously found the kitchen. He cringed. What colour was avocado anyway? He was too scared to look.

Cassidy reappeared, one of her hands dripping wet, both perched at her waist. 'Kitchen's not too bad.' She swept her eyes around the room again, the smile automatically reappearing on her face. She walked over and sat down on the sofa next to Brad, giving his knee a friendly tap. 'Well, it has to be said, this place is spotlessly clean. And the shower's working.' She lifted her nose and sniffed the air. 'And it smells as if the carpets have just been cleaned. See—it's not so bad.'

Not so bad. She had to be joking.

And she was. He could see her shoulders start to shake again. She lifted her hands to cover her face, obviously trying to block out the laughter. His stomach fell even further.

'What is it?'

He could tell she was trying not to meet his gaze. 'Go on. What else have you discovered in this psychedelic temple of doom?' He threw up his hands.

Cassidy stood up and grabbed his hand, pulling him towards her. For a second he was confused. What was she doing? Sure, this had crossed his mind, but what did she have in mind?

She pulled him towards the other room he hadn't looked at yet—the bedroom. Surely not? He felt a rush of blood to the head and rush of something else to the groin. This couldn't be happening.

She pushed open the door to the room, turning and giving him another smile. But the glint in her eyes was something else entirely. This was no moment of seduction. This was comedy, through and through.

He stepped inside the bedroom.

Pink. Everywhere and everything. Pink.

Rose-covered walls. A shiny, *satin* bedspread. Pink lampshades giving off a strange rose-coloured hue around the room. Pink carpet. Dark teak furniture and dressing table. He almost expected to see an eighty-year-old woman perched under the covers, staring at them.

Cassidy's laughter was building by the second. She couldn't contain herself. She spun round, her hands on his chest. 'Well, what do you think? How's this for a playboy palace?'

His reaction was instantaneous. He grabbed her around the waist and pulled her with him, toppling onto the bed, the satin bedspread sliding them along. He couldn't help it. It was too much for him and for the next few minutes they laughed so hard his belly was aching.

They lay there for a few seconds after the laughter finally subsided. Brad's eyes were fixed on the ceiling, staring at yet another rose-coloured light shade.

He turned his head to face Cassidy's. 'So, tell me truthfully. Do you think this flat will affect my pulling power?'

Cassidy straightened her face, the laughter still apparent in her eyes. She wondered how to answer the question. Something squeezed deep inside her. She didn't want Brad to have pulling power. She didn't want Brad to even consider pulling. What on earth was wrong with her? She'd only met this guy today. Her naughty streak came out. 'Put it this way. This is the first time I've lain on a bed with a man, panting like this, and still been fully dressed.'

His eyebrows arched and he flipped round onto his side to face her. 'Well, Sister Rae, that almost sounds like a challenge. And I like a challenge.'

Cassidy attempted to change position, the satin bedspread confounding her and causing her to slide to the floor with a heavy thud.

Brad stuck his head over the edge of the bed. 'Cass, are you okay?'

She held up her hand towards him and shook her head. 'Just feed me.'

Fifty boxes later and another trip back to the hospital, they both sagged on the sofa. Brad pulled a bunch of take-away menus from a plastic bag. 'I'd take you out for dinner but I don't think either of us could face sitting across a table right now.'

Cassidy nodded. She flicked through the menus, picking up her favourite. 'This pizza place is just around the corner and it's great. They don't take long to deliver. Will we go for this?'

'What's your favourite?'

'Thin crust. Hawaiian.'

'Pineapple—on a pizza? Sacrilege. Woman, what's wrong with you?'

She rolled her eyes. 'Don't tell me—you're a meat-feast, thick-crust man?'

He sat back, looking surprised. 'How did you know?'

'Because you're the same as ninety per cent

of the other males on the planet. Let's just order two.' She picked up the phone, giving it a second glance. 'Wow, my parents had one of these in the seventies.' She listened for a dial tone. 'Never mind, it works.' She dialled the number and placed the order.

'So, what do you think of your new home? Will you still be talking to Frank in the morning?'

Brad sighed. 'I think I should be grateful, no matter how bad the décor is. I needed a furnished flat close by—it's not like I had any furniture to bring with me   so this will be fine.' He took another look around. 'You're right—it's clean. That's the most important thing.' Then he pointed to Bert in the corner. 'And if he's happy, I'm happy.' The wicked glint appeared in his eyes again. 'I can always buy a new bedspread—one that keeps the ladies on, instead of sliding them off.'

There it was again. That little twisting feeling in her gut whenever he cracked a joke about other women. For the first time in a lifetime she was feeling cave-woman primal urges. She wanted to shout, *Don't you dare!* But that would only reveal her to be a mad, crazy person, instead of the consummate professional she wanted him to think she was.

He rummaged around in a plastic bag at his

feet. 'I'm afraid I can't offer you any fancy wine to drink. I've got orange or blackcurrant cordial.' He pulled the bottles from the bag. 'And I've got glasses in one of those boxes over there.'

Cassidy reached over and opened the box, grabbing two glasses and setting them on the table. 'So what's your story? What are you doing in Scotland?' *And why hasn't some woman snapped you up already?*

'You mean, what's a nice guy like me doing in a place like this?' He gestured at the psychedelic walls.

She shrugged. 'I just wondered why you'd left Australia. Do you have family there? A girlfriend?' She couldn't help it. She really, really wanted to know. She'd wanted to ask if he had a wife or children, but that had seemed a bit too forward. He wasn't wearing a wedding ring, and he hadn't mentioned any significant other. And he'd been flirting with her. Definitely flirting with her. And for the first time in ages she felt like responding.

'I fancied a change. It seemed like a good opportunity to expand my experience. Scottish winters are notorious for medical admissions, particularly around old mining communities.' He paused for a second and then added, 'And, no, there's no wife.' He prayed she hadn't noticed the hesitation. He couldn't say the words 'no children'. He wouldn't lie about his daughter. But he just didn't want to go there right now. Not with someone he barely knew.

Cassidy nodded, sending silent prayers upwards for his last words, but fixed her expression, 'There's around two and half thousand extra deaths every winter. They can't directly link them to the cold. Only a few are from hypothermia, most are from pneumonia, heart disease or stroke. And last year was the worst. They estimated nine pensioners died every hour related to the effects of the cold. Fuel payments are through the roof right now. People just can't afford to heat their homes. Some of the cases we had last year broke my heart.'

Brad was watching her carefully. Her eyes were looking off into the distance—as if she didn't want him to notice the sheen across her eyes when she spoke. He wondered if she knew how she looked. Her soft curls shining in the dim flat light, most of them escaping from the ponytail band at the nape of her neck. It was clear this was a subject close to her heart—she knew her stuff, but as a sister on a medical receiving unit he would have expected her to.

What he hadn't expected was to see the

compassion in her eyes. Her reputation was as an excellent clinician, with high standards and a strict rulebook for the staff on her ward. But this was a whole other side to her. A side he happened to like. A side he wanted to know more about.

'So, what's the story with you, then?'

She narrowed her eyes, as if startled he'd turned the question round on her. 'What do you mean?'

'What age are you, Cassidy? Twenty-seven? Twenty-eight?' He pointed to her left hand. 'Where's your other half? Here you are, on a Monday night at…' he looked at his watch '…nearly nine o'clock, helping an orphaned colleague move into his new flat. Don't you have someone to go to home to?'

Cassidy shifted uncomfortably. She didn't like being put on the spot. She didn't like the fact that in a few moments he'd stripped her bare. Nearly thirty, single and no one to go home to. Hardly an ad for Mrs Wonderful.

'I'm twenty-nine, and I was engaged a few years ago, but we split up and I'm happy on my own.' It sounded so simple when she put it like that. Leaving out the part about her not wanting to get out of bed for a month after Bobby had left. Or drinking herself into oblivion the month after that.

His eyebrows rose, his attention obviously grabbed. 'So, who was he?'

'My fiancé? He was a Spanish registrar I worked with.'

'Did you break up with him?'

The million-dollar question. The one that made you look sad and pathetic if you said no. Had she broken up with him? Or had Bobby just told her he was returning to Spain, with no real thought to how she would feel about it? And no real distress when she'd told him she wouldn't go with him.

Looking back she wondered if he'd always known she wouldn't go. And if being with her in Scotland had just been convenient for him—a distraction even.

She took a deep breath. 'What's with the questions, nosy parker? He wanted to go home to Spain. I wanted to stay in Scotland. End of story. We broke up. He's back working in Madrid now.' She made it sound so simple. She didn't tell him how much she hated coming home to an empty house and having nobody to share her day with. She didn't say how whenever she set her single place at the table she felt a little sad. She didn't tell him how much she hated buying convenience meals for one.

'Bet he's sorry he didn't stay.'

Cassidy's face broke into a rueful smile and she shook her head. 'Oh, I don't think so. He went home, had a whirlwind romance and a few months later married that year's Miss Spain. They've got a little son now.'

She didn't want to reveal how hurt she'd been by her rapid replacement.

He moved a little closer to her. 'Didn't that make you mad? He left and played happy families with someone else?'

Cassidy shook her head determinedly. She'd had a long time to think about all this. 'No. Not really. I could have been but we obviously weren't right for each other. When we got engaged he said he would stay in Scotland, but over time he changed his mind. His heart was in Spain.'

Her eyes fell downwards for a few seconds as she drew in a sharp breath, 'And I'd made it clear I didn't want to move away. I'm a Scottish girl through and through. I don't want to move.'

Brad placed his hand on her shoulder. 'But that seems a bit off. Spain's only a few hours away on a plane. What's the big deal?'

Cassidy looked cross. He made it all sound so simple. 'I like it here. I like where I live. I don't want to move to…' she lifted her fingers in the air '…*sunnier climes.* I want to stay here…' she pointed her finger to the floor '…in Scotland, the country that I love. And I have priorities here—responsibilities—that I couldn't take care of in another country.' She folded her arms across her chest.

'So I made myself a rule. My next other half will be a big, handsome fellow Scot. Someone who wants to stay where I do. Not someone from the other side of the planet.'

The words hung between them. Almost as if she was drawing a line in the sand. Brad paused for a second, trying to stop himself from saying what he really thought. Should he say straight away that he would never stay in Scotland either? That he wanted his life to be wherever his daughter was—and he was prepared to up sticks and go at a moment's notice?

No. He couldn't. That would instantly kill this flirtation stone dead. And that's all this would ever be—a mild flirtation. Why on earth would what she'd just said bother him? He was merely looking for a distraction— nothing more. Something to take his mind off another Christmas without his daughter.

'Just because someone is from Scotland it doesn't mean they'll want to stay here. There have been lots of famous Scots explorers— David Livingstone, for example.' He moved forward, leaning in next to her. 'Anyway, that's a pretty big statement, Cassidy. You're ruling out ninety-nine per cent of the population of the world in your search for Mr Right. Hardly seems fair to the rest of us.' He shot her a cheeky grin. 'Some people might even call that a bit of prejudice.'

'Yeah, well, at least if I think about it this way, it saves any problems later on. I don't want to meet someone, hook up with them and fall in love, only to have my heart broken when they tell me their life's on the other side of the planet from me.' *Been there. Done that.* 'Why set myself up for a fall like that?'

'Why indeed?' He'd moved right next to her, his blue eyes fixed on hers. She was right. Cassidy wanted to stay in Scotland. Brad wanted to go wherever in the world his little girl was. A little girl he hadn't even told her about. Anything between them would be an absolute disaster. But somehow he couldn't stop the words forming on his lips.

'But what happens if your heart rules your head?' Because try as he may to think of her as a distraction, the attraction between them was real. And it had been a long time since he'd felt like this.

She could see every tiny line on his face from hours in the Australian sun, every laughter line around the corners of his eyes. His hand was still resting on her arm, and it was making her tingle. Everything about this was wrong.

She'd just spelled out all the reasons why this was so wrong. He was from Australia. The other side of the planet. He was the worst possible option for her. So why, in the space of a day, was he already getting under her skin? Why did she want to lean forward towards his lips? Why did she want to feel the muscles of his chest under the palms of her hands? He was so close right now she could feel his warm breath on her neck. It was sending shivers down her spine.

She didn't want this to be happening. She didn't want to be attracted to a man there was no future with. So why couldn't she stop this? Why couldn't she just pull away?

*Ding-dong.*

Both jumped backwards, startled by the noise of the bell ringing loudly. Even Bert awoke from his slumber and started barking.

Cassidy was still fixed by his eyes, the shiver continuing down her spine. A feeling of awakening. 'Pizza,' she whispered. 'It must be the pizza.'

'Saved by the bell,' murmured Brad as he stood up to answer the door. At the last sec-

ond he turned back to her. A tiny little part
of him was feeling guilty—guilty about the
attraction between them, guilty about not
mentioning his daughter, and completely irritated by her disregard for most of the men
in the world.

Her mobile sounded, and Cassidy fum-
bled in her bag. 'Excuse me,' she murmured,
glancing at the number on the screen.

She stepped outside as he was paying for
the pizzas and pressed the phone to her ear.
'Hi, it's Cassidy Rae. Is something wrong
with my grandmother?'

'Hi, Cassidy. It's Staff Nurse Hughes here.
Sorry to call, but your gran's really agitated
tonight.'

Cassidy sighed. 'What do you need me to
do?' This was happening more and more.
Her good-natured, placid gran was being
taken over by Alzheimer's disease, at times
becoming confused and agitated, leading to
outbursts of aggression that were totally at
odds with her normal nature. The one thing
that seemed to calm her down was hearing
Cassidy's voice—whether over the phone or
in person.

'Can you talk to her for a few minutes? I'll
hold the phone next to her.'

'Of course I will.' She took a deep breath.

'Hi, Gran, it's Cassidy. How are you feeling?' Her words didn't matter. It was the sound and tone of her voice that was important. So she kept talking, telling her gran about her day and her plans for the week.

And leaving out the thoughts about the new doctor that were currently dancing around in her brain.

Brad sat waiting patiently. What was she doing? Who was she talking to outside in that low, calm voice? And why couldn't she have taken the call in here?

More importantly, what was *he* doing?

Getting involved with someone he worked with hadn't worked out too great for him the last time. He'd had a few casual dates in the last year with work colleagues, but nothing serious. He really didn't want to go down that road again.

So what on earth was wrong with him? His attraction to this woman had totally knocked him sideways. Alison had been nothing like this. A few weeks together had proved they weren't compatible. And the pregnancy had taken them both by surprise. And although his thoughts had constantly been with his daughter, this was the first time that a woman had started to invade his mind.

His brain wasn't working properly, but his libido was firing on multiple cylinders. Which one would win the battle?

# CHAPTER THREE

*11 October*

CASSIDY'S fingers hammered on the keyboard, responding to yet another bureaucratic email.

'What's up, girl?' As if by magic, Brad was leaning across the desk towards her. 'You've got that ugly frown on your face again. That usually spells trouble for the rest of us.'

Cassidy smiled. For the last ten days, every time she'd turned around he'd been at her elbow. His mood was generally laid-back and carefree, though a couple of times she'd thought he was going to steer a conversation toward something more serious. She turned the computer monitor towards him. 'Look at this. According to "customer care" principles, we've got to answer the ward phone on the third ring.'

'Since when did our patients become "customers"?'

'Oh, don't get me started. I just replied, pointing out that patients are our first priority on the medical unit and I won't be leaving a patient's bedside to answer the phone in three rings.'

'Are you still short-staffed?' Brad looked around the ward, noting the figures on the ward and trying to work out if everyone was there.

Cassidy pointed to the board. 'There were seven staff sick last week, but they should all be back on duty either today or tomorrow.' Her frown reappeared. 'Why, what are you about to tell me?'

Brad walked around to her side of the desk and wheeled her chair towards him. 'I was going to invite you to breakfast. It's Saturday morning, the ward's pretty quiet, so it seemed like a good time.' He pulled a face. 'Plus, those five empty beds you've got are about to be filled. I've got five patients coming into A and E via the GP on-call service who will all need to be admitted.'

Cassidy stood up. 'So what's this, the calm before the storm?'

'Something like that. Come on.' He stuck his elbow out towards her. 'You'll probably not get time for lunch later.'

Cassidy handed over the keys to one of her

staff nurses and headed down to the canteen with Brad.

There was something nice about this. The easy way they'd fallen into a friendship. She'd mentioned her front door was jamming and he'd appeared around at her flat to fix it. Then they'd walked to the Botanic Gardens a few times on days off and taken Bert out in the evenings. Even though they were tiptoeing around the edges of friendship, there was still that simmering 'something' underneath.

'I see you actually managed to put some clothes on today.' She ran her eyes up and down his lean frame, taking in his trousers and casual polo shirt. 'I was beginning to wonder if you actually owned any clothes.'

They'd reached the canteen and Brad picked up a tray. 'It's a deliberate ploy. If I live my life in scrubs then the hospital does my laundry for me. And I haven't got my washing machine yet.'

Cassidy nodded. 'Ah...the truth comes out.' She walked over to the hot food and lifted a plate. 'Why didn't you just say? You could have used my washing machine.'

'You'd do my washing for me?'

Cassidy shuddered. 'No. I said you could *use* my washing machine. I didn't say *I* would do it for you. Anyway, that's one of my rules.'

He watched as she selected a roll, put something inside and picked up a sachet of ketchup.

'What do you mean—one of your rules?'

She lifted a mug and pressed the button for tea. 'I have rules. Rules for the ward, rules for life, rules for men and rules for Christmas.'

He raised his eyebrows. 'Okay, now you've intrigued me. Either that, or you're a total crank—which is a distinct possibility.' He picked up his coffee. 'So, I'm interested. I know about the rules for the ward but tell me about these rules for men.'

She handed over her money to the cashier and sat down at a nearby table. 'They're simple. No overseas men.'

'Yeah, yeah. I've heard that one. And I'm not impressed. What else?'

'No washing. No ironing. No picking up after them. I'm not their mother. Do it a few times and they start to expect it. I get annoyed, then I start picturing them as Jabba the Hut, the fat, lazy monster from *Star Wars*, and yadda, yadda, yadda.' She waved her hand in the air.

'I was right. You *are* a crank.' He prodded her roll. 'And what is that? Everyone around here seems to eat it and I've no idea what it is.'

'It's slice.'

'Slice? A slice of what?'

'No. That's what it's called—slice. It's square sausage. A Scottish delicacy.'

'That's not a sausage. That looks nothing like a sausage.'

'Well, it is. Want to try a bit?' She held up her roll towards him.

He shook his head. 'That doesn't look too healthy. Apart from the pizza the first night I met you, you seem to spend your life eating salads or apples. I've never even seen you eat the sweets on the ward.'

'But this is different. This is Saturday morning. This is the bad-girl breakfast.' She had a twinkle in her eye as she said it.

Brad moved closer, his eggs abandoned. 'Should I keep a note of this for future reference?'

There it was again—that weird little hum that seemed to hang in the air between them. Making the rest of the room fall silent and fade away into the background. Making the seconds that they held each other's gaze seem like for ever.

But he kind of liked that. He kind of liked the fact that she didn't seem to be able to pull her gaze away any more than he could. He kind of liked the fact that once he was in the vicinity of Cassidy, his brain didn't seem to be able to focus on anything else. And from right here he could study the different shades of brown in her eyes—some chocolate, some caramel, some that matched her chestnut hair perfectly.

*Whoa!* Since when had he, Brad Donovan, ever thought about the different shades of colour in a woman's eyes? Not once. Not ever. Until now. Where had his brain found the words 'chocolate', 'caramel' and 'chestnut'?

'Maybe you should.' The words startled him. There it was again, something in the air. The way at times her voice seemed deeper, huskier, as if she was having the same sort of thoughts that he was.

But what did she think about all this? Was he merely a distraction? After all, she didn't want a man from the other side of the world; she wanted a Scotsman. And he clearly wasn't that. So why was she even flirting with him?

But now her eyes were cast downwards, breaking his train of thought. There was a slight flush in her cheeks. Was she embarrassed? Cassidy didn't seem the bashful type. Maybe she was having the same trouble he was—trying to make sense of the thoughts that seemed to appear as soon as they were together.

He didn't like silence between them. It

seemed awkward, unnatural for two people who seemed to fit so well together.

He picked up his fork and started eating his eggs. 'So, tell me about the Christmas rules?'

Cassidy sat back in her chair, a huge smile appearing on her face in an instant. Her eyes went up towards the ceiling. 'Ah, Christmas, best time of year. I love it, absolutely love it.' She counted on her fingers. 'There are lots of rules for Christmas. You need to have a proper advent calendar, not the rubbish chocolate kind. You need the old-fashioned kind with little doors that open to pictures of mistletoe and holly, sleighs, presents and reindeer. Then your Christmas tree needs to go up on the first of December.' She pointed her finger at him. 'Not on the twelfth or Christmas Eve, like some people do. You need to get into the spirit of things.'

'Should I be writing all this down?'

'Don't be sarcastic. Then there's the presents. You don't put them under the tree. That's a disaster. You bring them out on Christmas Eve.'

Brad was starting to laugh now. The enthusiasm in her face was brimming over, but she was deadly serious. 'Cassidy, do you still believe in Santa Claus?'

She sighed. 'Don't tell me you're a Christmas Grinch. There's no room for them in my ward.'

The Christmas Grinch. Actually, for the last few years, it would have been the perfect name for him. It was hard to get into the spirit of Christmas when you didn't know where your little girl was. Whether she was safe. Whether she was well. Whether she was happy. Cassidy did look literally like a child at Christmas. This was obviously her thing.

He tried to push the other thoughts from his mind. He was trying to be positive. This year he wasn't going to fall into the black hole he'd found himself in last year, dragged down by the parts of his life he couldn't control.

'Any other Christmas rules you need to tell me?'

'Well, there's all the fun stuff. Like trying to spot the first Christmas tree someone puts up in their window. I usually like to try and count them as I walk home from work every day. Then trying to guess who has got your name for the secret Santa at work. And the shops—I love the shops at Christmas. The big department store on Buchanan Street has the most gorgeous tree and decorations. They'll be up in a few weeks. You have to go and see them. And there will be ice skating in George Square. We have to go to that!'

'But it's still only October. We haven't had Hallowe'en yet.' Brad took a deep breath. He had an odd feeling in the pit of his stomach.

'We celebrate Christmas in Australia, too, you know. It might be a little different, but it's every bit as good as it sounds here. Where I live in Perth, everyone has Christmas lights on their houses. We have a huge Christmas tree in Forrest Place that gets turned on every November. Okay—maybe the temperature is around forty degrees and we might spend part of the day on the beach. But it's still a fabulous time. I'm gutted I won't be there this year.'

He was pushing his Christmas memories aside, and curiosity was curling at the bottom of his stomach. Little pieces of the puzzle that was Cassidy Rae were clicking into place. 'Have you ever celebrated Christmas anywhere else?'

Cassidy shook her head fiercely. 'I couldn't for a minute imagine being anywhere other than here at Christmas. Sometimes it even snows on Christmas Eve and Christmas Day. Then it's really magical.'

Brad frowned. 'Didn't you even celebrate Christmas in Spain with your fiancé?'

Cassidy looked at him as if he had horns on his head. 'Absolutely not.'

He folded his arms across his chest. 'Surely it doesn't matter where you celebrate Christmas—it's about who you celebrate with. It's the people, Cass, not the place.' He willed his voice not to break as he said the words. She would have no idea how much all this hurt him.

Cassidy was still shaking her head, and Brad had the distinct feeling he'd just tiptoed around the heart of the matter. She didn't want to move. She didn't want to leave. She wouldn't even consider moving anywhere else.

In some circumstances it might seem fine, patriotic even. But it irritated Brad more than he wanted to admit. How could Cass be so closed-minded? Was this really why she wouldn't even consider a relationship with him? Not that he'd asked her. But every day they were growing closer and closer.

Why hadn't he told her about Melody yet? The most important person in his life and he hadn't even mentioned her existence. He'd heard from his lawyer yesterday. Still no news. Still no sign. America was a big place. They were searching every state to see if Alison had registered as a doctor, though by now she could be married and working under a different name. If that was the case, they might never find her. And that thought made him feel physically sick.

His brain was almost trying to be rational now. Trying to figure out why Alison hadn't contacted him.

He was a good father—committed to Melody and her upbringing. He'd wanted a say in everything and that had kind of spooked Alison, who liked to be in control. And if she'd really met someone and fallen in love, he could almost figure out why she'd done things this way.

If she'd told him she wanted to move to the US, there would have been a huge custody battle. But to steal his daughter away and let eighteen months pass with no contact? That, he couldn't understand—no matter what.

He almost wanted to shout at Cassidy, *It's the people, Cass—always the people.* He couldn't care less where he was in this world, as long as he was near his daughter.

His mind flickered back to the four tightly packed boxes stuffed in the bottom of the wardrobe in his bedroom. Eighteen months of his life, with a private investigator in Australia and one in the US. Eighteen months when almost all his salary had gone on paying their fees and jumping out of his skin every time the phone rang.

No one could keep living like that. Not even him. It destroyed your physical and mental health. So he'd tried to take a step back, get some normality back into his life. He was still looking for his daughter and still had a private investigator in the US. But now he didn't require a daily update—an email once a week was enough. And the PI was under strict instructions to phone only in an emergency.

He looked at the woman across the table. He still couldn't get to the bottom of Cassidy Rae. She'd received another one of those phone calls the other day and had ducked out the ward, talking in a low, calm voice.

What on earth was going on?

Cassidy stared across the table. Maybe she'd gone a little overboard with the Christmas stuff. She always seemed to get carried away when the subject came up. It looked as if a shadow had passed across Brad's eyes. Something strange. Something she didn't recognise. Was it disappointment? She drew her breath in, leaving a tight feeling in her chest. She didn't like this.

But she didn't know him that well yet. She didn't feel as if she could share that it was just her and her gran left. And she wanted to hold on to what little family she had left. Of course Christmas was about people—even if they didn't know you were there.

She reached across the table and touched his hand. Every single time she touched him it felt like this. A tingle. Hairs standing on end. Delicious feelings creeping down her spine. The warmth of his hand was spreading through her.

He looked up and gave her a rueful smile, a little sad maybe but still a smile.

'Let's talk about something else. Like Hallowe'en. We usually have a party for the staff on the ward. I had it in my flat last year, but I think yours would be the perfect venue this time.'

Brad's smile widened. He looked relieved by the change of subject. 'I guess a Hallowe'en party wouldn't be out of the question in the House of Horrors.'

'It's not a House of Horrors. Why don't we just tell people we've got a theme for the year? It could be Hallowe'en-slash-fancy-dress, 1960s-style?'

He nodded slowly. 'I suppose we could do that. Are you going to help me with the planning?'

'Of course.' Cassidy stood up and picked

up her plate and mug, 'Come on, it's time to go back upstairs. We can talk about it as we go.'

He watched her retreating back and curvy behind. One thing was crystal clear. This woman was going to drive him crazy.

*30 October*

Brad opened the door as yet another party reveller arrived. Bert had retreated to his basket, now in Brad's pink bedroom, in sheer horror at the number of people in the small flat. It seemed that inviting the 'medical receiving unit' to a party also included anyone who worked there, used to work there or had once thought about working there.

It also included anyone who'd ever passed through or seen the sign for the unit.

'Love the outfit!' one of the junior doctors shouted at Brad. He looked down. Cassidy had persuaded him to go all out, and his outfit certainly reflected that. The room was filled with kipper ties, psychedelic swirls, paisley patterns, and mini-skirts and beehives. For the men, stick-on beards seemed to be the most popular choice, with lots of them now sticking to arms, foreheads and chests.

Brad pushed through the crowd to the

kitchen, finding an empty glass and getting some water. It was freezing outside, but inside the flat he almost felt as if he were back in Perth. He'd turned the cast-iron radiators off, but the place was still steaming, even with the windows prised open to let the cold air circulate.

He felt someone press at his back. 'Sorry, it's a bit of a squash in here.' He recognised the voice instantly.

'Where have you been? Wow!' Cassidy had helped him carry all the food and drink for the party up to the flat. Then she'd disappeared to get changed. His eyes took in her short red *Star Trek* dress, complete with black knee-high boots and gold communicator pinned to her chest. She pressed the button. *'How many to beam aboard?'*

'You didn't tell me we were doing TV. Not fair. How come you get to look smart and sexy and I get to look like some flea-bitten wino?'

She laughed and moved forward. 'I'm still in the sixties. The first episode of *Star Trek* was screened in 1966. I'm in perfect time.'

Someone pressed past her and she struggled to keep her glass of wine straight, moving so close to Brad that their entire bodies were touching. Her eyes tilted upwards towards him. 'I kind of like your too-tight shirt and shaggy wig. It suits you in a funny way.'

'Well, that outfit definitely suits you. But I feel as if you've fitted me up. I bet you had that sexy fancy-dress outfit stashed somewhere and were just looking for an excuse to give it an outing.' His broad chest could feel her warm curves pushing against him.

'You think I look sexy?' Her voice was low again and husky. Her words only heard by him. Someone else pushed past and she moved even closer in the tiny kitchen. *'How many to beam aboard?'*

They jumped. Startled by the noise. Brad grabbed her hand and pulled her through the door, past the people in the sitting room dancing to Tom Jones and the Beatles, and into the pink bedroom, pushing the door closed behind them.

Cassidy let out a little gasp. The pink shiny bedspread was gone, replaced by a plain cotton cream cover and pillowcases. But the dark pink lampshades hadn't been replaced, leaving a pink glow around the room. 'Too many people falling off your bed?'

He pulled the wig from his head, revealing his hair sticking up in all directions. 'Now, why would you think that?' There was a smile on his face as he stepped closer, pushing her against the door. His eyes were fixed on hers. His hand ran up her body, from the top of her boot, touching the bare skin on her legs, past the edge of her dress to her waist.

'Why would something like that even occur to you, Cass? Why would it even enter your mind? Because you keep telling me that we're friends. Just friends. You don't want anything more—not with someone like me, someone from Australia.' *Or someone with a missing child.*

Cassidy's heart was thudding against the inside of her chest. From the second he'd closed the door behind them she'd been picturing this in her head. No. Not true. From the first day that she'd met him she'd been picturing this in her head. It had taken her two glasses of wine to have the courage to come back to his flat tonight.

The tension had built in the last few weeks. Every lingering glance. Every fleeting touch sending sparks fluttering between them. It didn't matter how much her brain kept telling her he was the wrong fit. Her body didn't know that. And it craved his touch.

This wasn't meant to be serious. Serious had been the last thing on her mind—particularly with a man from overseas. But even though she tried to push the thoughts aside,

Brad was rapidly becoming more than just a friend. She loved the sexual undercurrent between them, and the truth was she wanted to act on it. Now.

She leaned forward, just a little. Just enough to push her breasts even closer to him. If he looked down, all he would be able to see now was cleavage. *'How many to beam aboard?'* The noise startled both of them, but Brad only pulled her closer. She reached up and pulled the communicator badge from her dress, tossing it onto the bed behind them. 'I hate it when the costume takes away from the main event.'

She could see the surprise in his eyes. He'd expected a fight. He'd expected her to give him a reason why he shouldn't be having the same thoughts she was.

She smiled, her hand reaching out and resting on his waist. 'Sometimes my body sends me different messages from my brain.'

Brad lifted a finger, running it down the side of her cheek. The lightest touch. Her response was immediate. Her face turned towards his hand, and his fingers caught the back of her head, intertwining with her hair. She leaned back into his touch, letting out a little sigh. Her eyes were closed, and she could feel his stubble scraping her chin, his warm breath near her ear. 'And which message are you listening to?' he whispered as his other hand slid under her dress.

'Which one do you think?'

She caught his head in her hands and pulled his lips towards hers. This was what she'd been waiting for.

His lips touched hers hungrily, parting quickly, his tongue pushing against hers. She wrapped her arms around his neck.

This was it. Stars were going off in her head. If he didn't keep doing this she would explode. Because everything about this felt right. And it was just a kiss—right? Where was the harm in that?

'I've waited a whole month to kiss you,' he whispered in her ear.

'Then I've only got one thing to say—don't stop.'

# CHAPTER FOUR

*2 November*

'WHAT are you doing here?'

It was three o'clock in the morning, and the voice should have startled her, but it didn't; it washed over her like warm treacle.

She turned her head in the darkened room where she was checking a patient's obs, an automatic smile appearing on her face. 'I got called in at eleven o'clock. Two of the night-shift staff had to go home sick, and it was too late to call in any agency staff.' She wrinkled her nose. 'Sickness bug again. What are you doing here? I thought Franco was on call.'

Brad rolled his tired eyes. 'Snap. Sickness bug, Franco phoned me half an hour ago with his head stuck down a toilet.'

Cassidy nodded. 'Figures. This bug seems to hit people really quickly. Loads of the staff are down with it. Let's just hope we manage to avoid it.' She finished recording the obs in the patients chart and started walking towards the door. Brad's arm rested lightly on her waist, and although she wanted to welcome the feel of his touch, it just didn't seem right.

'No touching at work,' she whispered.

His eyes swept up and down the dimly lit corridor. 'Even when there's no one about? Where's the fun in that?' His eyes were twinkling again, and it was doing untold damage to her flip-flopping stomach. She stopped walking and leaned against the wall.

'It's like this, Dr Donovan.' She moved her arm in a circular motion. 'I'm the master of all you can survey right now, and it wouldn't do to be caught in a compromising position with one of the doctors. That would give the hospital gossips enough ammunition for the rest of the year.' She looked down the corridor again, straightening herself up, her breasts brushing against his chest.

'I may well be the only nurse on duty in this ward right now, but I've got a reputation to maintain.' She tapped her finger on his chest. 'No matter how much men of a dubious nature try to waylay me.'

Brad kept his hands lightly resting on her waist. 'Hmm, I'm liking three o'clock in the morning, Cassidy Rae. It sounds as if there might be a bit of a bad girl in there.' He had that look in his eye again—the one he'd had when he'd finally stopped kissing her a few nights ago. The one that suggested a thousand other things they could be doing if they weren't in the wrong place at the wrong time. 'We really need to improve our timing.'

He was grinning at her now. The tiny hairs on her arms were starting to stand on end. This man was infectious. Much more dangerous than any sickness bug currently sweeping the ward.

She could feel the pressure rising in her chest. How easy would it be right now for them to kiss? And how much did she want to? But it went against all her principles for conduct and professional behaviour. So why did they currently feel as if they were flying out the window?

No matter how she tried to prevent it, this man had got totally under her skin. She was falling for him hook, line and sinker. No matter how much her brain told her not to.

She tried to break the tension between them. 'What do you want, anyway? I didn't page you. Shouldn't you be in bed?' The irony of the words hit her as soon as they left her mouth, her cheeks automatically flushing.

Brad and bed. Two words that should never be together in a sentence. The images had haunted her dreams for the last few nights. And she had a very *active* imagination.

His fingers tugged her just a little closer so he could whisper in her ear. 'Bed is exactly where I'm planning on being. But not here. And not alone.'

Cassidy felt her blush intensify. Was she going to deny what had been on her mind? She wasn't normally shy around men. But something about Brad was different. Something was making her cautious.

And she wasn't sure what it was. She couldn't quite put her finger on it yet. But as long as she had the slightest inclination what it was, she didn't want to lose her heart to this guy. No matter how irresistible he was.

'I've got two patients coming up. Two young guys who've—what is it you call it here?—been out on the lash?'

Cassidy laughed and nodded at his phrasing. He really was trying to embrace the Scottish words and phrases around him. She raised her eyebrows, 'Or you could call them *blootered*.'

Brad shook his head. 'I think you all deliberately wait until I'm around and start using all these words to confuse me.' He looked out the window into the night at the pouring rain. 'One of the other nurses down in A and E called the two young guys *drookit* and *mauchit*. I have no idea what she was talking about.'

Cassidy laughed even harder. 'Look outside, that will give you a clue. *Drookit* is absolutely soaking. *Mauchit* means really dirty. I take it the guys were found lying on the street?'

Brad nodded. 'I'm getting the hang of this, though. It's...' he lifted his fingers in the air '...going like a fair down there.'

She laughed. 'See—you're learning. Bet you hadn't heard that expression before you came to Scotland.' Her brow wrinkled. 'Hang on, where is it going like a fair? In A and E?'

'The short-stay ward is full already. That's why you're getting these two. They'll need Glasgow coma scale obs done. Are you okay with that?'

Cassidy smiled. 'Of course I am. We're used to getting some minor head injuries on the ward on a Saturday night.' She walked over to the filing cabinet and pulled out the printed sheets, attaching them to two clipboards for the bottom of the beds. She turned to face him. 'You know a group of doctors at one of the local hospitals invented this over thirty years ago.' She waved the chart at him. 'Now it's used the whole world over. One of the doctors is still there. He's a professor now.'

Brad raised his eyebrows. 'Aren't you just the little fund of information at three in the morning?' He looked around again. 'Haven't you got some help? I'm not happy about you being here alone with two drunks. There's no telling how they'll react when they finally come round.'

Cassidy pointed to a figure coming down the corridor. 'Claire, the nursing auxiliary, is on duty with me. She was just away for a break. And if I need help from another staff nurse, I can call through to next door.'

She turned her head as she heard the lift doors opening and the first of the trolleys being pulled towards the ward. 'Here they come.' She scooted into the nearby six-bedded ward and pulled the curtains around one of the beds.

Five minutes later a very young, very drunk man was positioned in the bed, wearing a pair of hospital-issue granddad pyjamas. Cassidy wrinkled her nose at the vapours emanating from him. 'Phew! He smells like a brewery. I could get anaesthetised by these fumes.' She spent a few moments checking his blood pressure and pulse, checking his limb movements and trying to elicit a verbal and motor response from him. Finally she drew her pen torch from her pocket and checked his pupil reactions.

She shook her head as she marked the observations on the chart. 'At least his pupils are equal and reactive. He's reacting to pain, but apart from that he's completely out of it.' She checked the notes from A and E. 'Any idea of a next of kin?'

Brad shook his head. 'Neither of the guys had wallets on them. This one had a student card in his pocket but that was it.'

He raised his head as the rattle of the second trolley sounded simultaneously to his pager going off. He glanced downwards at the number. 'It's A and E again. Are you sure you're okay?'

Claire had joined her at the side of the bed. 'We'll be fine, but just remember, there are no beds left up here.'

Brad nodded. 'I'll try to come back up later,' he said as he walked down the corridor towards the lift.

Cassidy spent the next hour doing neurological observations on the two patients every fifteen minutes. Both of them started to respond a little better, even if it was belligerently. It was four o'clock in the morning now—that horrible time of night for the night shift where the need to sleep seemed to smack them straight in the head. Her eyes were beginning to droop even as she walked the length of the corridor to check on her patients. Sitting down right now would be lethal—she had to keep on the move to stay awake.

A monitor started pinging in one of the nearby rooms. 'I'll get it,' she shouted to Claire. 'The leads have probably detached again.'

She walked into the room of Mr Fletcher, a man in his sixties admitted with angina. Every time he'd turned over in his sleep tonight, one of the leads attached to his chest had moved out of place.

Cassidy flicked on the light, ready to silence the alarms on the monitor. But Mr Fletcher's leads were intact. His skin was white and drawn, his lips blue and his body rigid on the bed. The monitor showed a rapid, flickering electrical line. Ventricular fibrillation. His heart wasn't beating properly at all. Even though the monitor told her what she needed to know, she took a few seconds to check for a pulse and listen for breathing.

'Claire!' She pulled the red alarm on the

wall, setting off the cardiac-arrest procedure as she released the brake on the bottom of the bed and pulled the bed out from the wall. She removed the headrest from the top of the bed and pulled out the pillows. Claire appeared at her side, pulling the cardiac-arrest trolley behind her. 'I've put out the call.' She was breathing heavily.

Cassidy took a deep breath. Brad was the senior doctor carrying the arrest page tonight. If he was still down in A and E, it would take him at least five minutes to get up here. Glasgow City Hospital was an old, sprawling building, with bits added on over time. It hadn't been designed with emergencies in mind, like some of the modern, newly built hospitals were. The anaesthetist would probably take five minutes to get here, too.

It didn't matter what the monitor said. Cassidy took a few seconds to do the old-fashioned assessment of the patient. Airway. Breathing. Circulation. No pulse. No breathing.

'Start bagging,' she instructed Claire, pointing her to the head of the bed and handing her an airway as she connected up the oxygen supply to the ambu-bag. She turned the dial on the defibrillator, slapping the pads on

Mr Fletcher's chest and giving it a few seconds to pick up and confirm his rhythm.

'Stand clear,' she shouted to Claire, waiting a few seconds to check she'd stood back then looking downwards to make sure she wasn't touching the collapsed metal side rails. She pressed the button and Mr Fletcher's back arched upwards as the jolt went through his body.

Her adrenaline had kicked in now. She didn't feel sleepy or tired any more. She was wide awake and on alert, watching the monitor closely for a few seconds to see if the shock had made any impact on his heart rhythm. Nothing. Still VF.

The sound of feet thudded down the corridor as Brad appeared, closely followed by one of the anaesthetists. Brad's eyes widened as he realised who the patient was. 'VF,' she said as they entered the room. 'I've shocked him once at one hundred and twenty joules.' Even though she had only been back on the ward for a month, she was on autopilot.

'What happened?' asked Brad. 'He was pain free earlier and we had him scheduled for an angiogram tomorrow.'

'Alarm sounded and I found him like this,' she said. 'He hadn't complained of chest pain at all.' She raised her knee on the bed and positioned her hands, starting the chest compressions. The anaesthetist took over from Claire and within a few seconds inserted an endotracheal tube. Cassidy continued the cycles of compressions as Brad pulled the preloaded syringes from the crash cart. After five cycles she stopped and their heads turned to the monitor again to check the rhythm.

'I'm giving him some epinephrine,' Brad said as he squirted it into the cannula in the back of Mr Fletcher's hand. 'Let's shock him again.' He lifted the defibrillator paddles. 'Stand clear, everyone. Shocking at two hundred joules.'

Everyone stood back as Mr Fletcher's body arched again. Cassidy went to resume the compressions. They continued for the next ten minutes with cycles of compressions, drugs and shocking. Cassidy's arms were starting to ache. It was amazing how quickly the strain of doing cardiac massage told on shoulders and arms.

'Stop!' shouted Brad. 'We've got a rhythm.' He waited a few seconds as he watched the green line on the monitor. 'Sinus bradycardia.'

He raised his eyes from the bed. 'Cassidy, go and tell Coronary Care we're transferring a patient to them.'

She ran next door to the coronary care unit, and one of their staff members came back through with her, propping the doors open for easy transfer. They wheeled the bed through to the unit and hooked Mr Fletcher up to the monitors in the specially designed rooms. In a matter of a few moments, he was safely installed next door.

Cassidy nodded at Brad as she left him there to continue Mr Fletcher's care. Claire gathered up his belongings and took them next door while Cassidy quickly transferred him on the computer system.

She took a deep breath and heaved a sigh of relief. The adrenaline was still flooding through her system, her arms ached and her back was sore.

Claire appeared with a cup of steaming tea, which she put on the desk in front of her. 'Okay, Cassidy? I nearly jumped out of my skin when that alarm sounded. He'd been fine all night.'

Cassidy nodded. 'I hate it when that happens. Thank goodness he was attached to a cardiac monitor. I dread to think what would have happened if he hadn't been.'

A loud groan sounded from the room opposite the nurses' station. Cassidy stood back up. 'No rest for the wicked. That will be one of our head-injury patients.'

Sure enough, one of the young men was starting to come round. Cassidy started checking his obs again, pulling her pen torch from her pocket to make sure his pupils were equal and reactive. His score had gradually started to improve as he could obey simple instructions and respond—albeit grudgingly. Hangovers didn't seem to agree with him.

She moved on to the patient next door, who still appeared to be sleeping it off. As she leaned over to check his pupils, his hand reached up and grabbed her tunic. 'Get me some water,' he growled, his breath reeking of alcohol and his eyes bloodshot.

Cassidy reacted instantly, pushing him backwards with her hands to get out of his grasp. 'Don't you dare put a hand on me,' she snarled.

'Cass.' The voice was instant, sounding behind her as Brad sidestepped around her, filling the gap between her and the patient.

The sunny surfer boy with cheerful demeanour was lost. 'Don't you dare touch my staff.' He was furious, leaning over the patient.

The drunken young man slumped back

against the pillows, all energy expended. 'I need some water,' he mumbled.

Brad grabbed hold of Cassidy's hand and pulled her beyond the curtains. He ran his fingers through his hair. 'He still requires neuro obs, doesn't he?'

Cassidy nodded. 'That's the first time he's woken up. His neuro obs are scheduled to continue for the next few hours.'

Brad marched over to the phone and spoke for a few moments before putting it back down. 'I don't want you or Claire going in there on your own. Not while there's a chance he's still under the influence of alcohol and might behave inappropriately. Somebody from Security will be up in a few minutes and will stay for the rest of the shift.'

He walked into the kitchen and picked up a plastic jug and cup, running the tap to fill them with water. 'I'll take him these. You sit down.'

Cassidy didn't like anyone telling her what to do, especially in her ward. But for some reason she was quite glad that Brad had been around. It wasn't the first time a patient had manhandled her—and she was quite sure it wouldn't be the last. But there was something about it happening in the dead of night, when there weren't many other people around, that unsettled her.

And as much as she wanted to fly the flag for independence and being able to handle everything on her own, she was quite glad one of the security staff was coming up to the ward.

Brad appeared a moment later, walking behind her and putting his hands on her taut neck and shoulders. He automatically started kneading them with his warm hands. 'You okay, Cass?'

For a second she was still tense, wondering what Claire might think if she saw him touching her, but then relaxing at his touch. Her insides felt as tight as a coiled spring. What with the cardiac massage and the reaction of her patient, this was exactly what she needed. She leaned backwards a little into his touch.

'Right there,' she murmured as he hit a nerve. 'How's Mr Fletcher doing?'

Brad's voice was calm and soothing. 'He's in the right place. The staff in Coronary Care can monitor him more easily, his bradycardia stabilised with a little atropine and his blood pressure is good. We've contacted his family, and he'll be first on the list in the morning. He'll probably need a stent put in place to clear his blocked artery.'

'That's good. Mmm…keep going.'

'Your muscles are like coiled springs. Is this because of what just happened?'

She could hear the agitation in his voice.

'I hate people who react like that. How dare they when all we're trying to do is help them? He could have died out there, lying on the street with a head injury, getting battered by the elements. It makes my blood boil. If I hadn't come in when I did…' His voice tailed off then he leaned forward and wrapped his arms around her neck—just for a second— brushing a light kiss on her cheek.

It was the briefest of contacts before he straightened up, reaching for the cup of tea Claire had made a few minutes earlier and setting it down on the desk in front of her. 'Drink this.' He folded his arms and sat down in the chair next to her, perching on the edge. 'I need to go back to Coronary Care. What are you doing on Sunday? Want to grab some lunch?'

Cassidy hesitated, her stomach plunging. She had plans on Sunday. Ones she wasn't sure about including Brad in. After all, he was just a fleeting moment in her life, a 'passing fancy', her gran would have said. She wasn't ready to introduce him to her family yet. Especially in her current circumstances.

But the hesitation wasn't lost on Brad. 'What's up? Meeting your other boyfriend?' he quipped.

Her head shook automatically. 'No, no.' Then a smile appeared. 'What do you mean, my *other boyfriend*? I wasn't aware I had a boyfriend right now.' Why did those words set her heart aflutter? This wasn't what she wanted. Not with a man from thousands of miles away. Not with someone who would leave in less than a year. So why couldn't she wipe the smile off her face?

He could see the smile. *Distraction.* Was that all that Cass was? What about how'd he had felt a few minutes ago when that drunk had touched her? The guy was lucky there hadn't been a baseball bat around. Cass was getting under his skin. In more ways than one. And it was time. Time to tell her about Melody.

It would be fine. He'd tell her on Sunday. She would understand. She would get it. He had other priorities. He wanted to find his daughter, and that could take him anywhere in the world. Cassidy would be fine about it. She didn't want a serious relationship with an Australian. She obviously didn't mind the flirtation and distraction. Maybe she wouldn't even mind a little more. Something more inevitable between them.

This wasn't anything serious—she would know that. But he just didn't want anyone else near her right now.

Brad stood back up. 'Well, you do. So there.' He planted another kiss firmly on her cheek. 'And whatever you're doing on Sunday, plan on me doing it with you.' And with those words he strode down the corridor, whistling.

*7 November*

'We seem to be making a habit of this.' Brad smiled at Cassidy, his mouth half-hidden by the scarf wrapped around his neck, as she turned the key in the lock of the little terraced house in the East End of Glasgow.

His leather-gloved hand was at her waist and his body huddled against hers. It was freezing cold and the pavements already glistening with frost. Cassidy pushed the door open and stepped inside. 'I'm afraid it's not much warmer inside. Gran hasn't lived here for over a year, and I have the heating on a timer at minimum to stop the pipes from freezing.'

Brad pushed the door shut behind him,

closing out the biting wind. 'I can't believe how quickly the temperature's dropped in the last few days. I've had to buy a coat, a hat and a scarf.'

Cassidy stepped right in front of him, her chestnut curls tickling his nose. 'And very nice you look, too.'

He leaned forward and kissed the tip of her nose, before rubbing his gloved hands together. 'So what happens now?'

She led him into the main room of the house and pointed at some dark teak furniture. 'The van should be here any time. It's taking the chest of drawers and sideboard in here, the wardrobe in Gran's bedroom and the refrigerator from the kitchen. The furniture goes to someone from the local homeless unit who's just been rehoused.'

'I take it there's no chance your gran will ever come home.'

Cassidy shook her head fiercely, and he could see a sheen cross her eyes. 'No. She fell and broke her arm last year. It was quite a bad break—she needed a pin inserted. She's already suffered from Alzheimer's for the past few years. I'd helped with some adaptations to her home and memory aids, but I guess I didn't really understand how bad she was.'

Cassidy lifted her hands. 'Here, in her

own environment, she seemed to be coping, but once she broke her arm and ended up in hospital...' Her voice trailed off and Brad wrapped his arm around her shoulders.

'So where is she now? Was there no one else to help her? Where are your mum and dad?'

'She's in a nursing home just a few miles away. And it's the second one. The first?' She shuddered, 'Don't even ask. That's why I agreed to the secondment. It meant I could spend a bit more time helping her get settled this time. Her mobility is good, but her memory is a different story—some days she doesn't even know who I am. Other days she thinks I'm my mother. I can't remember the last time she knew I was Cassidy. And now she's started to get aggressive sometimes. It's just not her at all. The only thing that helps is hearing my voice.'

The tears started to spill down her cheeks. 'I know I'm a nurse and everything but I just hate it.' Brad pulled his hand from his glove and wiped away her tears with his fingers.

He nodded slowly. So that's what the telephone calls had been about. No wonder she'd wanted some privacy to take them. 'So where's your mum and dad? Can't they help with your gran?'

Cassidy rolled her eyes. 'My mum and dad are the total opposite of me. Sometimes I feel as if I'm the parent and they're the children in this relationship. Last I heard, they were in Malaysia. They're engineers, dealing with water-pumping stations and pipelines. They basically work all over the world and hardly spend any time back here.'

His brow furrowed. He was starting to understand Cassidy a little better. Her firm stance about staying in Scotland was obviously tied into feeling responsible for her gran. 'So you don't get much support?'

She shook her head.

'Is there anything I can do to help?'

Cassidy looked around her. The pain was written all over her face. 'Everything in this house reminds me of Gran. I packed up her clothes last month and took them to the Age Concern shop.' She walked over to a cardboard box in the corner of the room, filled with ornaments wrapped in paper, crinkling the tissue paper between her fingers. 'This all seems so final.'

The knock at the door was sharp, startling them both. Ten minutes later almost all the heavy furniture had been loaded onto the van by two burly volunteers. 'The last thing is in here.' Cassidy led them into the bedroom and pointed at the wardrobe. She stood back as the two men tilted the wardrobe on its side to get it through the narrow door. There was a clunk and a strange sliding noise.

Brad jumped forward. 'What was that? You emptied the wardrobe, didn't you, Cassidy?'

She nodded. 'I thought I had.'

He pulled open the uptilted wardrobe door and lifted up a black plastic-wrapped package that had fallen to the floor. 'You must have missed this.'

Cassidy stepped towards him and peered inside the wardrobe. 'I can't imagine how. I emptied out all the clothes last month. I was sure I got everything.' She turned the bulky package over in her hands. 'I don't know how I managed to miss this.' She gave the men a nod, and they continued out the door towards the van.

Brad thanked the men and walked back through to the bedroom. Cassidy was sitting on the bed, pulling at the plastic wrapper. There was a tiny flash of red and she gave a little gasp.

'Wow! I would never have expected this.' She shook out the tightly wrapped red wool coat and another little bundle fell to the floor. Cassidy swung the coat in front of the mirror. The coat was 1940s-style, the colour much brighter than she would have expected, with black buttons and a nipped-in waist.

'This coat is gorgeous. But I can't *ever* remember Gran wearing it. I don't even think I've seen a picture of her in it. Why on earth would she have it wrapped up at the back of her wardrobe? It looks brand new.'

Brad knelt on the floor and picked up the other package wrapped in brown paper. 'This was in there, too. Maybe you should have a look at them?'

Cassidy nodded and then gave a little shiver.

'Let's go to the coffee shop at the bottom of the road. It's too cold in here. We'll take the coat with us,' he said.

She headed through to the kitchen and pulled a plastic bag from under the sink, carefully folding the red coat and putting it inside. 'This coat feels gorgeous.' She held the edge of it up again, looking in the mirror at the door. 'And I love the colour.'

'Why don't you wear it?' Brad could see her pupils dilate, just for a second, as if she was considering the idea.

She shook her head. 'No. No, I can't. I don't know anything about it. I don't even know if it belonged to Gran.'

'Well, I think it would look perfect on you,

with your dark hair and brown eyes. Red's a good colour for you. Did you inherit your colouring from your gran?'

Cassidy still had her fingers on the coat, touching it with a look of wistfulness in her eyes. 'I think so. I've only ever seen a few photos of her when she was a young girl. She was much more glamorous than me.'

Brad opened the front door as the biting wind whirled around them. He grabbed her hand. 'I've got a better idea. Why don't we get a coffee to go and just head back to my flat? It's freezing.'

Cassidy nodded as she pulled the door closed behind them and checked it was secure. They hurried over to the car and reached his flat ten minutes later, with coffee and cakes from the shop round the corner from him.

Although it was only four o'clock, the light had faded quickly and the street was already dark. 'Look!' screamed Cass. 'It's the first one!'

Brad dived to rescue the toppling coffee cups from her grasp. 'What is it?' His head flicked from side to side. 'What on earth are you talking about?'

'There!' Her eyes were lit up and her smile reached from ear to ear. He followed Cassidy's outstretched finger pointing to a flat positioned across the street above one of the shops. There, proudly displayed in the window, was a slightly bent, brightly lit-up Christmas tree.

'You have got to be joking. It's only the seventh of November. Why on earth would someone have their Christmas tree up?'

He couldn't believe the expression of absolute glee on her face. She looked like a child that had spotted Santa. 'Isn't it gorgeous?'

And there it was. That horrible twisting feeling inside his stomach. The one he was absolutely determined to avoid this year. That same empty feeling that he felt every year when he spent the whole of the Christmas season thinking about what he'd lost, what had slipped through his fingers.

He felt the wind biting at his cheek. Almost like a cold slap. Just what he needed. This year was going to be different. He'd done everything he possibly could. It was time to try and get rid of this horrible empty feeling. He'd spent last Christmas in Australia, the one before that in the US, following up some useless leads as to Alison and Melody's whereabouts.

This year would be different. That was part of the reason he'd come to Scotland. A country that had no bad memories for him. A chance to think of something new.

Cassidy's big brown eyes blinked at him in the orange lamplight. She'd pulled a hat over her curls and it suited her perfectly. 'I really want to put my tree up,' she murmured. 'But it's just too early.' She looked down at the bustling street. 'Only some of the shops have their decorations up. I wish they all had.'

This was it. This was where it started. 'Christmas means different things to different people, Cass. Not everyone loves Christmas, you know?'

He saw her flinch and pull back, confusion in her eyes. There was hesitation in her voice. 'What do you mean? Is something wrong? Did something happen to you at Christmas?'

He hesitated. How could he tell her what was currently circulating in his mind? He wasn't even sure he could put it into coherent words. Melody hadn't disappeared at Christmas, but everything about the season and the time of year just seemed to amplify the feelings, make them stronger. Most importantly, it made the yearning to see his daughter almost consume him. He blinked. She was standing in the dimmed light, her big brown eyes staring up at him with a whole host of questions.

He should tell her about Melody, he really should. But now wasn't the time or the place. A shiver crept down his spine as the cold Scottish winter crept through his clothes. A busy street filled with early festive shoppers wasn't the place to talk about his missing daughter.

And no matter how this woman was currently sending electric pulses along his skin, he wasn't entirely sure what he wanted to share. He wasn't sure he was ready.

'Brad?' Her voice cut through his thoughts, jerking him back to the passing traffic and darkened night.

He bent forward and kissed the tip of her nose, sliding his arm around her shoulders. 'Don't be silly, Cass. Nothing happened to me at Christmas.' He shrugged his shoulders as he pulled her towards him, guiding her down the street towards his flat. 'I'm just mindful that lots of the people we see in the hospital over Christmas don't have the happy stories to share that you do.'

She bit her lip, cradling the coffee cups and cakes in her arms as she matched his steps along the busy street. 'I know that. I didn't just materialise onto the medical unit from a planet far away. I've worked there a long time.'

But her words seemed lost as his steps lengthened and he pushed open the door to the close ahead of them.

Cassidy took off her bright blue parka and put it on the sofa. She'd seen something in his eyes. Almost as if a shadow had passed over them, and it had made her stomach coil. Was there something he wasn't telling her?

She pulled the coffee cups from their holder and opened the bag with the carrot cake inside. This was exactly what she needed right now. The sofa sagged next to her as Brad sat down. He was still rubbing his hands together.

'I can't believe how cold it is out there.'

She smiled at him. 'Get used to it—this is only the start. Last year it was minus twelve on Christmas Day. My next-door neighbour is a gas engineer and his phone was ringing constantly with people's boilers breaking down.' She picked up the cup and inhaled deeply. 'Mmm. Skinny caramel latte. My favourite in the world. I haven't had one of these in ages.' She took a tiny sip then reached for the moist carrot cake.

'So I take it the fact you have a *skinny* caramel latte counteracts the effects of the carrot cake?'

She winked at him. 'Exactly.' She raised

her eyes skywards. 'Finally, a man on my wavelength. They cancel each other out. And it's a skinny caramel latte with sugar-free syrup. Which means I can enjoy this all the more.' She licked the frosting from the carrot cake off the tips of her fingers.

'With this...' she nibbled a bit from the corner. '...a girl could think she was in heaven.'

'I can think of lots of other ways to put a girl in heaven,' the voice next to her mumbled.

Cassidy froze. Her second sip of coffee was currently stuck in her throat. You couldn't get much more innuendo than that. Should she respond? Or pretend she hadn't heard?

There was no denying the attraction between them. But did she really want to act on it? After a month in his company, what did she really know about Brad Donovan? She could give testimony to his medical skills and his patient care. He was amenable, well mannered and supportive to the staff.

But what did she really know about him? Only little snippets of information that he'd told her in passing. Stories about home in Australia, living in Perth and his training as a doctor. Passing remarks about childhood friends. He'd told her he had no wife or girlfriend.

So what else was it? What had made that dark shadow pass in front of his eyes? Why had he hesitated before answering the question? Or had she just imagined it all? Maybe there was nothing wrong, maybe something had caught his eye at the other side of the road, momentarily distracting him and stopping him from answering the question.

In the meantime, she could still feel that underlying buzz between them. Whenever he was near, she had visions of that night in his flat, pressed up against the wall in her sci-fi costume, wishing things could go further than they had.

Every time he touched her at work, even the merest brush of a hand was enough to set off the currents between them. It didn't matter that her head told her this wasn't sensible—he came from the other side of the world and would likely return there; her body was telling her something entirely different. Her imagination was telling her a whole host of other things…

He gave her a nudge, passing her the package he'd wedged under his jacket.

She stared down at the still-wrapped parcel in her hands, turning the brown paper package over and over.

'Are you going to open it?'

She picked at the tape in one corner. It was old, the stickiness long vanished, and it literally fell apart in her hands, revealing some white envelopes underneath. She pulled them out. Only they weren't white, they had yellowed with age, all with US postal stamps.

Her eyes lifted to meet his. Brad leaned forward, touching the pile of envelopes and spreading them out across the table. 'There must be at least twenty of them,' he said quietly. His fingers stopped at something. There, among the envelopes, was something else. A photograph. Brad slid the envelope that was covering it away and Cassidy let out a little gasp.

She leaned forward and picked up the black-and-white print. 'It's my gran!' she gasped. His head met hers as they stared at the photograph of a beautiful young woman with a smile that spread from ear to ear, wearing a beautiful coat with a nipped-in waist. Her head was turned to the side and her eyes were sparkling as she looked at the man standing next to her in a US army uniform.

Cassidy was stunned. There were a million thoughts that crowded into her mind. A million conclusions that she could jump to. But one thing stood out above all the rest. 'I've never seen her look so happy,' she whispered. 'Gran never looked like that.'

She turned to face Brad. 'I don't mean she was miserable—she was fine.' She pointed at the photograph. 'But I can't ever remember her looking like *that*.'

She didn't want to say anything else. She didn't know what to think. She'd just glimpsed a moment from the past, and it almost seemed sacred. The coat and letters had been hidden a long time ago by a woman who obviously hadn't wanted to throw them away but hadn't wanted them to be found. In a way, it almost felt like a betrayal.

She ran her finger over the photograph. 'I don't think I can even ask Gran about this. She's too far gone. I can't even remember the last time that she recognised me.'

Brad's arm wrapped around her shoulder. She could feel his breath at her neck. What would he be thinking? The same kind of thing that she was? That her gran had lost her heart to some US soldier?

She didn't want to think like that. It seemed almost judgemental. And it seemed wrong that Brad's first glimpse into her family was revealing something she hadn't known herself.

And she couldn't pretend that it didn't hurt

a little. It had been just her and Gran for the last ten years but she'd never told Cassidy anything about this. She'd been a modern woman, liberal-minded and easy to talk to. Why had she kept this to herself?

His voice was quiet and steady as he whispered in her ear. 'Don't even think about asking her about it, Cass.' He lifted the photograph from her hand and sat it back down on the table. 'Take it as it is. A happy memory from your gran's life. She's beautiful in that picture. You can see the happiness in her eyes. Why shouldn't she have had a time like that?' His finger ran down the side of her cheek. 'She looks a lot like you.'

Cassidy turned to face him. His mouth was only inches from hers and she subconsciously licked her lips. This was it. The moment she'd been waiting for.

It had taken him so long to kiss her again after the party. She didn't want to wait any longer. She didn't want to imagine any longer. She wanted to feel.

Her hands slid up around his neck as she pulled him closer. His mouth was on hers instantly, just the way she'd imagined. He pushed her backwards on the sofa, his hands on either side of her head as he kissed her, gently at first, before working his way down her neck, pushing her shirt open.

His body was warm, heating hers instantly. She could feel his whole length above her, and her hands moved from around his neck, down his back and towards his hips, pulling him closer to her.

This time there was no one else in the flat. This time they wouldn't need to stop. This time they could do what they wanted.

She pushed aside the rational side of her brain that was clamouring to be heard. She could worry about all that later. Her body was responding to him with an intensity she'd never experienced before. She'd already had a glimpse of the washboard abs when he'd changed in the doctors' office. Now she didn't just want to look—she wanted to touch, to feel, to taste.

He lifted his head, pushing himself back a little. His voice was little above a groan. 'Cass?'

The question only hung in the air for a fraction of a second. She didn't want to think about this. Right now she didn't care that he was from Australia and would probably go back there. Right now all she cared about was that he was here, *now*, with *her*.

A slow smile appeared on his face. 'Wanna stay over?'

He had no idea how sexy he was right now. His clear blue eyes were hooded with desire. She could feel his heart thudding against his chest. All for her.

She pressed herself against him again. 'I thought you'd never ask.'

He pulled her to her feet and led her towards his bedroom door, undoing the buttons on her shirt as they went. Her legs were on autopilot and she couldn't wipe the smile from her face.

He pressed her against the wall. 'I seem to remember being in this position with you before, Cassidy Rae.' His voice was deep, throaty, turning her on even more.

'I was playing hard to get,' she whispered in his ear. 'Did it work?'

He turned her around and pushed her onto the bed. 'Oh, yes.' He crawled towards her, poising himself above her. Her shirt was open now, leaving her breasts exposed in their black satin push-up bra. He bit at the edge with his teeth. 'Now, this doesn't look like ordinary underwear.' His fingers dug around her hips, sliding down the back of her jeans and finding the edge of her matching black g-string. 'Did you have something in mind when you got dressed this morning, Cass?' His low, sexy laugh sent shivers of delight down her spine.

It wasn't her normal underwear. But she could hardly even remember getting dressed this morning. Had she done this subconsciously, hoping she would end up in this position?

'Let's just say I'm a girl of many secrets.' She pulled his T-shirt over his head, revealing his pecs and tanned abdomen. If she hadn't been so turned on, she might have pulled in her stomach and worried about him seeing her curves. But from the look on his face, he liked what he was seeing. 'I have lots of gorgeous sets of underwear. If you're lucky, I'll let you see the red set,' she moaned as he started to kiss her neck, 'or the blue set...' Her hands were dipping lower on his body, to the front of his jeans where she could feel him throbbing against her. 'Or, if you're really lucky, I'll let you see the green set.'

He let out a groan. 'I can guarantee I'll love the underwear—no matter what colour. But what I love most is what's underneath. He traced his fingers down her throat as she arched her back in response. Then slid his hand underneath her, unfastening her bra strap and leaving her breasts exposed. 'Now, what can I do with these?' he murmured.

Cass pushed herself upwards, her breasts towards his mouth. 'You can start by getting rid of the rest of these clothes,' she commanded as she undid the buttons on his jeans, before wriggling out of her own. She waited as he discarded his jeans and underwear, before pushing him down on the bed and setting her legs astride him.

'I like this,' he murmured. 'A woman who likes to be in charge.'

'Oh, I'm always in charge,' she breathed in his ear as she ran her hands down his chest. 'And anyway, I'm examining your skin. You're way too tanned.' Her hands stopped at his nipples, brushing around them onto the fine hair on his chest. 'I feel it's my duty to check you for any areas of concern.' She lifted her hips and rubbed against him again.

He groaned. 'Anywhere in particular you'd like to start?'

She smiled and leaned over him again, her hardened nipples brushing against the skin on his chest. She swayed against him. 'I'll need to think about that.'

Brad let out a primal roar. He grabbed her and flipped her around on the bed so he was poised above her. 'Enough teasing. You're going to be the death of me.'

His fingers reached down and dispensed with her g-string. She could feel the heat rise inside her. She was aching for him. He touched her and she gasped, tilting her hips upwards to him. 'Oh…this is going to be so good.'

'You bet it is,' he whispered in her ear, the stubble on his jaw scraping her shoulder.

'Mmm… Where else am I going to feel that?'

'Wherever you like.'

He moved for a second, reaching into the nearby drawer, and she heard the rustle of a condom wrapper being opened. Ten seconds later he was above her again. 'Are you ready?' he whispered.

'Oh, yes…' She opened her legs further and gasped as he plunged inside her.

He stopped, just for a second. 'Okay?'

She took a deep breath, while the full sensation surrounded her. Then she pulled his hips even closer, taking him deeper inside. 'Don't you dare stop,' she groaned. 'I've got you just where I want you.'

'Ditto.' He smiled again as he moved slowly, building momentum between them as he trailed a line of kisses down the side of her face and throat.

And there it was—the fever that had been building between them for weeks. All the looks and lingering glances. All the brief touches. All the electricity buzzing around them like fireflies. The first kiss, with its strained finish. All building to this crescendo, where nothing and no one could get between them.

Cassidy could feel her skin start to tingle. Nothing else was more important than this. Nothing else had ever felt as good as this. Nothing else had ever felt this *right*. This was perfect.

She let herself go, throwing her head back and crying out his name, as she felt him stiffen at the same time.

She felt her body turn to jelly, the air whooshing out from her lungs. Brad was still above her, his whole body weight now resting on her, his heart thudding against her chest.

She let out a laugh. Sweat slicked them together as she gave him a playful push. 'Move, mister, I can hardly breathe.'

He pushed himself up and sagged down beside her.

'Wow.'

Cassidy was breathing heavily, her eyes

staring up at the ceiling and fixing on the still-pink light shade above her. She turned to the sandy-blond head on the pillow beside her, a smile creeping across her face. 'Yeah, wow,' she murmured.

# CHAPTER FIVE

*8 November*

THE early-morning Scottish light crept across the room. Even on the greyest days the sun's rays sneaked through the clouds and scattered this room with light. Brad's brain was fuzzy. Something was different. Something had changed.

Then he felt a movement beside him, and the memories of the night before crowded into his brain. Cassidy. Wow.

Then something else hit him, charging from the dark recesses of his brain, and he stifled the groan in his throat. Melody. He hadn't told her about Melody.

He turned around in the bed, resting his hand on his arm, staring at the sleeping figure beside him. Her chestnut curls spilled across the pillow that she had wedged half under her arm as she slept on her side, facing him.

She looked beautiful. Her fair skin was smooth and unlined. Cassidy. His distraction. The woman he'd lusted after for the last month.

But his stomach clenched. He was cringing. Things in his brain just didn't add up. If Cassidy was only a distraction, why should he tell her about Melody? There should be no need.

But he knew better than that. No matter how many times he tried to use the word 'distraction' for Cassidy, she was much more than that.

In the last few weeks she had crept under his skin. Hearing her voice brought a smile to his face. Knowing she was working the same shift made his whole day seem brighter. And spending time with her outside work made the days speed past. He knew her habits— she liked to take her shoes off at the door, she sat on the left-hand side of the sofa, she only watched the news on one TV channel. His mood had lifted just by being around her.

His thoughts were always with his daughter but they didn't consume every spare second of every day.

She made him happy. Cassidy made him happy. And he was about to jeopardise all that. He knew he should have told her about

Melody. He'd meant to but just hadn't found the appropriate time.

And now, after he'd slept with her, it seemed like a dirty secret. He almost wished he'd put a photo in the doctors' office in the ward as soon as he'd started there. But the truth was that office was used by lots of doctors and it wasn't appropriate to put a family picture in there. And he just hadn't been ready to answer any difficult questions about his daughter.

But now? He sagged back against the pillows. It looked as though he was hiding something. It looked as though he deliberately hadn't trusted Cassidy enough to tell her about Melody. How awkward was this conversation going to be?

He turned his head sideways to look at her again, to look at that perfect face before he ruined everything. A tiny part of him hoped that she wouldn't be annoyed at all. Maybe she would shrug her shoulders and tell him that it was fine?

Who was he kidding? How would he feel if the shoe was on the other foot? If Cassidy had a child she hadn't told him about? The thought was unimaginable. He could feel himself automatically shaking his head at the idea.

Things would be perfect if he could just

freeze this moment in time. Keep everything just the way it was right now. Or, even better, just the way they'd been last night. That thought sent a smile across his face. If only...

A frown appeared on Cassidy's brow then her eyelids flickered open. Those big brown eyes that pulled him in every time. A smile appeared on her face instantly. 'Morning,' she whispered.

Relief flooded through him. She hadn't woken up and panicked. She seemed happy and comfortable around him. She obviously had no regrets about the night before. Not yet, anyway.

'Morning,' he whispered back. He couldn't help it. He was immediately drawn to her. He wanted to touch her, taste her skin again. He dropped a kiss on the tip of her nose.

A glint appeared in her eyes. Memories of last night? 'Wow,' she whispered again, her soft breath on his face.

Brad couldn't hide the smile. Her memories were obviously as good as his. If only every morning could be like this.

Her hand crept around his neck, and as much as he wanted to pull her closer and forget about everything else, he just couldn't. He had to get this over and done with.

He shifted backwards in the bed. 'How

about I make you some breakfast?' His legs hit the floor before she had a chance to answer, and he pulled his underwear and jeans on rapidly. 'What would you like? Toast? Eggs? Bacon?'

Cassidy looked confused. She pushed herself upwards in the bed and adjusted the pillows behind her. 'I'll have whatever you're making,' she said quietly.

'Great. Give me five minutes and I'll give you a shout. Feel free to take a shower and freshen up.' He leaned forwards and planted another kiss on her forehead before disappearing out of the door.

Cassidy sat for a few minutes, taking deep breaths. What just happened? They'd had a fabulous night, and he'd asked her to stay over. And for a few seconds this morning when she'd woken up, everything had seemed fine. So what had made him jump out of bed like a scalded cat?

She flung back the duvet and swung her legs out of bed, wincing at the cold air in the room. There was a navy-blue dressing gown hanging up behind the bedroom door, and she wrapped it around herself, then headed to the bathroom.

She flicked the switch for the shower, grabbing an elastic band that was sitting on top

of the bathroom cabinet and twisting her hair
back from her face as she sat at the edge of
the bath for a few moments, trying to fathom
what was going on.

Was Brad regretting their night together?
The thought almost made her belly ache. She
couldn't imagine anything worse. Maybe he
was only interested in the thrill of the chase
and once that was over...

No. No, it couldn't be that. She'd got to
know him over the last few weeks, and he
didn't seem to be like that at all. Maybe he
just felt awkward because it was the first time
they'd woken up together?

Yes, that could be it. Her eyes fell to the
sink. Brad had obviously been in here first as
he'd left her a new toothbrush and toothpaste
and a huge white soft towel. She stuck her
hand under the shower. It had heated up perfectly, so she stepped into the steaming water.

There was almost a tremor on her skin. Her
insides were coiling, to the point of almost
feeling pain. She couldn't bear the thought of
Brad wanting to walk away after their night
together. And it wasn't about the humiliation
or about being used. Although those things
would be bad enough.

It would be the fact he didn't feel the same
connection that she did. The fact that his

thoughts didn't wander to her about a million times a day—the way hers did to him. It would be the fact he didn't feel the constant zing between them. Those were the things she couldn't bear.

She could still smell him on her skin and almost regretted having to wash it away, but the blue shower gel with its ocean scent reminded her of him again. She rubbed it into her body even harder, then a few minutes later stepped out of the shower and dried herself rapidly. It only took a few moments to realise she'd nothing to wear, so she padded back through to the bedroom and rummaged in a few of his drawers.

'Cassidy! Breakfast!'

The smell was drifting through the house. Eggs, bacon and tea. Perfect.

'Hey.'

She was standing in the doorway dressed in a pair of his grey jogging trousers and an oversized pale blue T-shirt. His clothes had never looked so sexy. Her hair was ruffled, some little strands around her neck still wet from the shower.

He pulled out a chair for her. 'Have a seat.' All Brad could think about right now was getting this over and done with. He had to come clean. Easier said than done.

He put the plates on the table and poured the tea while Cassidy watched him carefully. She wasn't stupid. She knew something was going on.

She took a sip of her tea, chasing her eggs around the plate with her fork. Watching. Waiting.

Brad pressed his lips together. He reached across the table and took her hand. 'Cass, there's something I need to tell you.'

He could see the tiny flare of panic in her eyes that she was trying to control. She set her tea back down on the table. Her voice was steady. 'So, what is it you want to tell me "the morning after the night before", Brad?'

He winced. There was no getting around this. Cassidy didn't even know what 'it' was—but the implication was there. If this was something important, he should have told her before he'd taken this relationship to the next level.

'I have a daughter.' The words were blurted out before he had a chance to think about it any longer.

'What?' The shocked expression on her face was very real. This was the last thing she'd expected to hear.

Brad took a deep breath. 'I have a daughter, Melody. She's nearly four.' His heart was beating against his chest, the words clambering to his mouth—he just couldn't speak quickly enough right now. 'I haven't seen in her over two years. Her mother, Alison, disappeared with her. We had a…' he flung his hands in the air '…sort of informal custody arrangement. Alison was a doctor as well, and we looked after Melody between us.'

Cassidy's face looked set in stone. 'She was your wife? Your girlfriend? The one you told me you didn't have?' Her tone said it all.

Brad spoke firmly. 'She wasn't my wife and she wasn't my girlfriend, well, not after a few months. We had a very short-lived fling that resulted in Melody. We'd broken up by the time Alison discovered she was pregnant, and neither of us were interested in getting back together.'

He leaned back in the chair, wishing he could tell the whole story in the blink of an eye. Everything about this was painful to him. Every time he spoke about things, he thought about the mistakes he had made and what he could have done differently.

Anything that could have affected the eventual outcome.

Cassidy hadn't moved. Her face was expressionless and her breakfast lay untouched in front of her.

'I don't really know what happened, Cass. I went to pick up Melody as arranged one day, and they were gone.' He flicked his hand in the air. 'Just like that. Vanished. I was frantic. I went to Alison's work and found out she'd resigned and no one knew where she'd gone. Some of her colleagues said she'd met a doctor from the US and been head over heels in love. They thought she might have gone to the US with him.' He shook his head as a wave of desperation swept over him. It was the same every time he spoke about this.

'I hired a lawyer and two private investigators and tried to track her down. I've been trying to track her down for the last two years—with no success. I haven't seen or heard from her in two years. Right now, I have no idea how my little girl is, where she is or if she even remembers me.' His eyes were fixed on the window, staring out into space.

Cassidy felt numb. 'You have a daughter,' she said.

He nodded, it appeared, almost unconsciously.

'You have a daughter you "forgot" to tell me about?' She couldn't help it—she raised her hands in the air and made the sign of quotation marks.

She could feel rage and anger bubbling beneath the surface, ready to erupt at any moment. She hadn't imagined anything the other night. It hadn't been all in her head. It had been right before her eyes—or it should have been.

Brad looked in pain. He may have been gazing outside, but the look in his eyes was haunted. A father who had lost his child. She couldn't begin to imagine the pain that would cause. But right now she couldn't contain her anger.

'Why didn't you mention this before?'

He sighed. A huge sigh, as if the weight of the world was on his shoulders. His gaze went to his hands that were clenched in his lap. 'I know, I know, I should have. But it just never felt like the right time.'

'How about as soon as you met me?'

His brow wrinkled. 'Oh, yeah. Right. Pleased to meet you, I'm Brad Donovan. I've got a missing daughter, Melody, that I've been searching for the last two years. And before you ask—no—I've no idea why her mother disappeared with her. No—I didn't do anything wrong or mistreat my child. Yes—I've spent an absolute fortune trying to find her and I've been on two wild-goose chases to the US.' He waved his hand in frustration. 'Is that how you wanted me to tell you?'

Cassidy took a deep breath. She wanted to yell. She wanted to scream. She could see how damaged he was by all this. But she couldn't see past how hurt she felt. Hadn't he trusted her enough to tell her? He trusted her enough to sleep with her—but not to tell her about his daughter? It seemed unreal.

She looked around, her eyes scanning the walls. 'So where are they?'

His brow furrowed. 'Where are what?'

She threw her hands up in frustration. 'The photos of your daughter. I've never seen a single one. Where do you keep them?'

He grimaced and stood up. She could hear him walking through to the living room and opening a drawer. He walked through and sat a wooden framed photograph down on the table.

Cassidy felt her heart jump into her mouth as she stared at the image in front of her. The gorgeous toddler with blonde ringlets and Brad's eyes was as pretty as a picture. She felt her lip tremble and she lifted her eyes to meet his. 'You put these away when you knew I would be here?'

He nodded. 'I planned to tell you.' He hesitated, having the good grace to look shame-faced. 'I just hadn't got around to it.'

'Why didn't you tell me when I first asked you about your family? When I asked you if you had a wife or a girlfriend? When I told you about my ex-fiancé and his new Miss Spain wife? How about telling me then? Correct me if I'm wrong, but wasn't that your ideal opportunity?'

She folded her arms across her chest. It didn't matter that she'd tried to play down how hurt she'd been over her breakup with her fiancé. The fact was she'd *told* him about it—albeit in sparing detail. There was no way he was getting away with this. She didn't care about the wonderful night before. She didn't care how many times he'd taken her to heaven and back.

This was about trust. This was about honesty. This was about the things you *should* tell someone before you slept with them.

Brad shook his head. 'You make it all sound so simple, Cass.'

She cringed. The exact thought she'd had when he'd asked her about Bobby. 'It is.'

'No. It's not.' His voice was determined. 'Okay, so you may have asked me about a wife or girlfriend—and I didn't have either, so I didn't tell you any lies. And I'd only just met you then, Cass. I don't want everyone to know my business, and this isn't the easiest thing to talk about. People talk. People make judgements.' He pressed his fingers against his temples.

'When Alison and Melody vanished at first, people were suspicious about me in Australia. People, colleagues even, wondered if I'd done something to them. It was only after the Australian police confirmed they'd left on an international flight that people stopped assuming I'd done something awful.'

Cassidy felt her heart constrict. It was something she hadn't even considered. It hadn't even entered her mind that someone would think like that about Brad. How could friends or colleagues have done that?

Her head was instantly filled with stories in the media, and after only a few seconds she realised it was true. As soon as anyone went missing, suspicion was generally directed at those around them. What on earth would that feel like?

She could only imagine the worst. The frustration of not knowing where your child was. Continually shouting but not being heard. It must have been excruciating.

He leaned his elbows on the table. His fingers moved in small circles at the side of his head. 'It didn't stop there either.' He lifted his head and stared at Cassidy. 'Once people realised I hadn't done something unmentionable to them, they started to say that Alison must have done a runner with Melody to get away from me. As if I'd done something to my child.'

The words hung in the air. Too hideous for thoughts even to form.

'Oh, Brad,' she breathed. Now she understood. Now she understood the pain in his eyes. 'That's awful.'

'You bet it is.'

A lump stuck in her throat. She was angry. She was hurt. And she had no idea what this could mean for them. But right now she had to show some compassion. She stood up, the chair scraping along the kitchen floor, and walked around to the other side of the table.

Brad looked as if he was in shock. As if he was wondering what she might do next.

She might never have had a child stolen from her, but she knew what it was like to be left.

Her parents had done it. Bobby had done it.

But she was calm and lifted his hands from the table, sitting down on his knee and wrapping her hands around his neck, hugging him closely. She could feel his tense muscles beneath her fingers, and she rubbed her hand across his back, waiting for a few moments until he relaxed and the pent-up strain had started to abate.

After a few minutes she leaned back, watching him carefully.

'I'm not happy, Brad. I can't believe you didn't tell me something as important as this.'

She felt him take a deep breath. Right now his blue eyes were almost a window into his soul. She could see his regret. She could see his pain. And although hers could only pale in comparison, she wondered if he could see hers.

'I didn't mean things to turn out like this. This wasn't in my plans.'

In an instant she could almost feel his withdrawal. The hackles rose at the back of her neck. 'What do you mean?'

His hands touched her waist. 'This. Us. I didn't realise things would get so serious.'

'What did you expect? You've practically spent the last five weeks by my side. Every time I turn around, you're right there next to me. If you didn't want us to be more than friends, you should have stayed away.' She hated how she sounded. She hated the tone of her voice, but she just couldn't help it.

The muscles on his shoulders tensed again

and he blew some hair from his forehead, obviously in exasperation. What on earth was he thinking? She had a hollow feeling in her stomach. After the wonderful night before, did he want to walk away?

Everything about this was confusing. She didn't even know how she felt about the fact he had a daughter—she hadn't had time to process those thoughts. Why was she even considering any of this? Her head had always told her this relationship was a bad idea. She wanted someone who would stay in Scotland with her, and the sinking feeling in her stomach told her Brad could obviously never do that.

But her body and soul told her something else entirely. Brad was the first man in a long time that she'd been attracted to—that she'd even been interested in. She loved spending time in his company. She loved his normally easygoing manner. She loved the fact she could depend on him at work—his clinical skills and judgement were excellent.

But most of all she loved the way she felt around him. Even yesterday, in her grandmother's house, doing a task that should have made her feel sad and depressed, there had been so much comfort from having Brad around.

And as for how her body reacted to him… that was something else entirely.

Brad reached up and touched her hair, winding his fingers through one of her curls. Her head tilted instantly—an automatic response—towards the palm of his hand. His eyes were closed. 'How could I stay away from this, Cass?'

He pulled her head down and touched a gentle kiss to her lips. 'You're like a drug to me, Cassidy Rae. Apart from Melody, you're the first thing I think about when I get up in the morning and the last thing I think about when I fall asleep at night.' His eyes opened and she could tell instantly he meant every word.

This was no gentle let-down. This was no attempt to look for an excuse to end their relationship. He was every bit as confused as she was.

She pulled back. This was too much. She was getting in too deep. She pushed herself upwards, her legs trembling as she walked around to the other side of the table and pushed her untouched plate of food away.

'I can't think when you do that. I can't think straight when you touch me. It's too distracting.'

Brad let out a short laugh, shaking his head.

'What? What is it?'

'That word, Cass—distraction. That's what I thought about you at first.'

Cassidy frowned. A distraction. Hardly a flattering description. But he reached across the table and touched her hand again.

'You have no idea how I was feeling when I got here. I'd just had the year from hell in Australia. I'd been to the US twice, chasing false leads trying to find Melody. None of them worked. I'd spent a fortune and still had no idea about my daughter. Last Christmas...' He raised his eyes to the ceiling.

'Let's just say it was the worst ever. Then a few of my friends sat me down and had a conversation with me that was hard for all us. They told me I should never give up looking for Melody, but I had to accept I had a life of my own to live. And they came prepared—they had an armful of job ads for all over the world. I'd let my career slide. I'd been consumed by doing everything I could to find my daughter. The job I'd always loved had become a noose around my neck. I didn't make any mistakes but I'd lost the enthusiasm and passion for the job.

'My friends knew the career paths I'd been interested in before, and they convinced me it was the right time for a break—a change of scenery and a time for new horizons.'

He gave her a rueful smile. 'I didn't come to Scotland with the intention of meeting anyone. I came to Scotland to experience the infamous Scottish winter and the ream of medical admissions that always follow. I planned to just immerse myself in work. To try and give myself a break from constantly checking my emails and phoning the private investigator in the US.'

Cassidy didn't know what to think. A distraction. That's what he'd just called her. She couldn't stop herself from fixating on it. And it gave her the strangest sensation—a feeling of panic.

Maybe this was it. Maybe she should grab her clothes— wherever they were— and get out of here. She needed time to think. She needed a chance to get her head around what he'd just told her. Right now she was suffering from information overload.

Her gaze drifted out the kitchen and onto the coffee table in the living room. She hated that word. It made her feel worthless. As if he didn't value her. The way Bobby had made her feel when he'd left. He'd never used that word, but that's the way she'd felt—as if he'd used her as a distraction, as if he hadn't valued her enough to stay. The same way her parents had made her feel. As if she wasn't worth coming home for.

The only person who hadn't made her feel like that had been Gran. Solid. Dependable. Warm and loving. But even that had changed now. Her gran was a mere shadow of her former self. And what about those letters? She really needed to sit down and decide what she wanted to do with them.

'Cass?'

She was startled. Brad's forehead was wrinkled. He'd still been talking to her, and she'd been lost in her own thoughts. 'What?' she answered quickly.

'You didn't hear me, did you?'

She shook her head. 'You've given me a lot to think about. Maybe I should leave? Maybe you don't need any more distractions.' Her mind could only focus on one thing and she stood up again, ready to leave.

But he was quicker than her, and it took him less than a second to have her in his arms. His face was just above hers. His stubbled jaw, tanned skin and blue eyes definitely distracted *her*.

'I said it was nice to meet someone who enjoyed Christmas so much. Last year is something I don't want to repeat. I was hoping you would help try to get me into the spirit.'

She blinked. He was using her weak spot. Her Christmas rush. And he was doing it with that lazy smile on his face and his fingers winding under her T-shirt.

She sighed. 'This isn't all just going to be okay. I'm going to need some time—to see how I feel.' Then the sticking point came to the forefront of her brain. 'And are you still just using me as a distraction?'

His head moved slowly from side to side. 'I'm not using you as anything. I just want to be around you, Cass. I have no idea where this is going to go. I have no idea what's going to happen between us. But I'd like to find out. What do you say?'

There it was. That feeling. For five weeks he'd made her feel special. Made her feel wanted and important—as if she were the centre of his life. She wanted to say a hundred things. She wanted to sit him down and ask more questions. But his fingers were trailing up her side...

'I need some time to think about all this, Brad. You certainly know how to spring something on a girl.'

He pulled back a little. 'I know, and I'm sorry. I should have told you about Melody.'

Right now she didn't know what to do. She'd learned more about Brad in the last fifteen minutes than she had in the last five weeks. He was hurt, he was damaged. She had seen that in his eyes. And for the last five weeks he'd come to work every day and been a conscientious and proficient doctor. Could she have done the same?

Who did he really have here as a friend? Who was there for him to talk to, to share with, apart from her?

More importantly, did she really want to walk away right now?

It would be the sensible thing to do. She was already feeling hurt, and walking away now could save her from any more heartache in the future. But she'd still need to work with him, she'd still see him at work every single day. How would she cope then? And how would she feel if she saw him with anyone else?

The thought sent a chill down her spine. She didn't want to see him with anyone else. In her head he was already *hers*. And even if this didn't go anywhere, why shouldn't she enjoy what they had right now? She certainly wouldn't mind a repeat of last night. The sooner, the better.

Her hands wound around his neck. 'How

about we try to create some new Christmas memories—some nice ones—ones that you could only experience here with me in Scotland?'

He nodded his head slowly. 'That sounds like a plan. What do I have to do in return?'

A thousand suggestions sprang to mind—most of them X-rated. She couldn't stand the pain she'd seen in his eyes earlier. But this definitely wasn't what she'd signed up for. She had to think about herself. She didn't want to end up hurt and alone. She didn't want to end up without Brad.

'I'm sure I'll think of something,' she murmured as she took him by the hand and led him back to the bedroom.

# CHAPTER SIX

*15 November*

CASSIDY hurried up the stairs. Her cardigan was useless this morning, and her new-style uniform wasn't keeping out the freezing temperatures. She touched one of the old-fashioned radiators positioned nearby the hallway. Barely lukewarm. That was the trouble in old stone buildings with antiquated heating systems; the temperature barely rose to anything resembling normal.

The true Scottish winter had hit with a blast over the last few days. This morning, on the way to work Cassidy had slipped and skidded twice on the glistening pavements. She dreaded to think what A and E had been like last night.

Brad had been on call, so she hadn't seen him. He'd phoned her once, around midnight, to say he was expecting a few admissions and to chat for a few minutes. But things had felt a little strained—just as they had for the last week. She still couldn't get her head around all this. Not least the part he hadn't told her he had a daughter.

But the thing she was struggling with most was how much she actually liked him. It didn't matter her head had told her he was ultimately unsuitable. For the last few weeks she'd spent every minute with him. And no matter how confused she was, one emotion topped the rest. She was happy.

Brad made her happy. Spending time with him made her happy. Talking to him every day made her happy. Working with him made her happy. Cuddling up on the sofa with him made her happy. Kissing made her *very* happy, and anything else...

Her heart sank as she saw the bright lights and bustling figures at the end of the corridor. It wasn't even seven o'clock in the morning and her normally darkened ward was going like a fair.

She strode into the ward, glancing at the board. Jackie, one of her nurses, came out of the treatment room, holding a medicine cup with pills and clutching an electronic chart.

'What's going on, Jackie?' She could see instantly that the normally cool and reliable member of staff looked frazzled. Jackie had worked nights here for over twenty years—it took a lot to frazzle her.

Jackie looked pale and tired, and she had two cardigans wrapped around her. 'What do you think?' She pointed at the board. 'I'll give you a full report in a few minutes, but we've had six admissions in the last few hours and we need to clear some beds—there are another four in A and E waiting to come up.'

Cassidy nodded quickly. 'What kind of admissions?'

Jackie pointed at the window to the still-dark view outside. 'All elderly, all undernourished, two with hypothermia and the other four all with ailments affected by the cold. Just what we always see this time of year.'

The stream of elderly, vulnerable patients reminded Cassidy of her gran.

'You rang?' Lucy appeared at Cassidy's side.

'I heard you needed to transfer four patients to my ward. Thought it would be easier if I just came along, got the report and then transferred them along myself.'

Cassidy nodded. 'Perfect.' She walked over to Jackie and took the medicine cup and electronic chart from her hands. 'Introduce me to this patient and I'll take over from you, then you can hand over to Lucy before we do the report this morning.'

Jackie nodded happily. 'That's great. If we get these patients transferred, I'll give you a proper handover before the beds get filled again.' She shrugged her shoulders. 'Brad's around here somewhere. I saw him a few moments ago. He hasn't stopped all night and…' she smiled '…our normally tanned doctor is looking distinctly pale this morning.' She winked at Cass. 'I hope he hasn't been having too many late nights.'

Cassidy froze. The words sank in quickly. She didn't think that anyone knew about Brad and herself. But she should have known better. Word always spread quickly in a hospital like this.

She tried to regain her composure and pretend she hadn't heard the comment—best not to make a big deal of these things and hope the gossip would disperse quickly.

Half an hour later, with the report given and Jackie quickly leaving to go home, Cassidy gave a sigh and went to make a cup of tea. The breakfast trolley had just rolled onto the ward. The auxiliary nurses and domestics were helping the patients, and her two staff nurses had started the morning drug round.

Lucy appeared at her side. 'Make one for

me, too, please. I've just taken the last patient round to my ward.'

Cassidy nodded and put two tea bags into mugs. She could kill for a skinny caramel latte right now.

Lucy nudged her. 'So, spill. What's happening with you and Dr Wonderful? I haven't seen you for over a week.'

Cassidy bit the inside of her lip. There was no point beating around the bush. Lucy would only pester her until she told anyway. She poured the boiling water into the cups.

Lucy nudged her again. 'Come on. Is the prediction going to come true? Are you going to be a Christmas bride?'

Cassidy dropped her teaspoon into the sink. 'What? Are you mad?' She'd forgotten all about smelly-cat woman and her mad predictions.

'What's wrong? I thought things were going swimmingly between you and surf boy. Come on, you must have done the dirty deed by now—surely?'

Cassidy felt the instant flush as the heat spilled into her cheeks. It was just a pity her body didn't know how to tell lies.

'I knew it! Well—tell all. Is he wonderful?'

She took a deep breath. 'Do you want me to answer everything at once?'

'I just want you to say something. Anything. What's wrong, Cass?'

'Well, in that case...' She counted off
on her fingers. 'No, I definitely won't be a
Christmas bride—and I'd forgotten all about
that rubbish. Yes, I've done the dirty deed.
Yes, it was wonderful—or it was until the
next day when he told me he had a daughter.'

'A daughter? Brad has a daughter?'

Cassidy nodded slowly.

'Why hasn't he ever mentioned her? What's
the big secret?'

Cassidy picked up her tea and leaned back
against the sink. 'The big secret is he doesn't
know where she is. Her mother vanished with
her two years ago. Apparently she fell in love
with some doctor from the US and didn't tell
Brad anything about it. He thinks she didn't
want to get into a custody battle with him, so
basically she did a moonlight flit.'

Lucy looked stunned and shook her head
slowly. 'Wow, he's a dark horse, isn't he? I
would never have guessed.'

Cassidy sighed again. 'Neither would I.'

There was silence for a few seconds. Lucy
touched her arm. 'Whoa, you've got it bad,
girl, haven't you?'

Cassidy closed her eyes. 'You could say
that.'

Lucy stepped in front of her, clutching her steaming cup of tea with one hand and wagging her finger with the other. 'What happened to Cassidy Rae and *"I'm never going to fall in love with another foreign doctor"*? Where did she go? And what's the big deal about Brad having a daughter? She's lost. The US is a big place, and chances are she might never be found.'

'Cassidy Rae met Brad Donovan. That's what happened. And as for his daughter, I've no idea what will happen. But one thing is for sure—ultimately he won't stay in Scotland with me.'

Lucy leaned forward and gave her a hug. 'Cassidy, you might be making a whole lot of something out of nothing.'

Cassidy stopped for a few moments. Maybe Lucy was right. He hadn't managed to find Melody so far—and that was with a private investigator working for him. Maybe he would never find her? Maybe she could just forget about Melody and start to focus on them again?

But she still had an uneasy feeling in her stomach. Brad wouldn't stay in Scotland—whether he found his daughter or not. Why on earth was she pursuing a relationship with a man who wasn't right for her?

She shook her head. 'A daughter isn't nothing, Lucy. It's a whole big something. What happens if we get serious, and then he gets a call to say his daughter has been found? I'll be left high and dry while he jets off somewhere to find his lost child. It's hardly the ideal setup for a lasting relationship.'

Lucy took a sip of her tea, watching Cassidy carefully. 'That's the first time I've ever heard you say anything like that.'

'Like what?'

'The whole words—"lasting relationship". I never even heard you say that about Mr Spain. You must really like our Dr Donovan.'

'I guess I do.' There. She'd said the words out loud. And to someone other than herself. It almost felt like a confession.

A little smile appeared at the corner of Lucy's mouth. 'That's what Lynn and I were talking about at Belinda the fortune-teller's house. We'd already pegged Brad for you and thought you'd make a nice couple.'

Cassidy stared at her as memories of that night and their knowing nods sprang up in her brain. 'You've got to be joking.'

Lucy shook her head, looking quite pleased with herself. 'No. We thought you'd be a good fit together. And we were right.'

Cassidy put down her mug and started to

fiddle with her hair clip. 'Well, you can't exactly say that now, can you?'

'Yes, I can. I still think you're a good fit.' She folded her arms across her chest. 'So what's been the outcome of Brad's big disclosure? Did you run screaming from the room? Have a tantrum? Go off in a huff?'

Cassidy lowered her head. 'That's just it. There's not really been an outcome. I'm still seeing him and we've talked about it a few times—but we've really only skirted around the edges.' She shrugged her shoulders. 'I've no idea what the big outcome will be.' She shook her head, 'I don't think he knows either.'

Lucy's brow puckered. She nipped Cassidy's arm. 'Who are you, and what have you done with the real Cassidy Rae? The one that always knows precisely what she, and everyone around about her, is doing?'

'Don't, Lucy. Don't remind me how much of an idiot I'm being.'

Lucy's face broke into a smile as she tipped the rest of her tea down the sink and rinsed her cup. 'I don't think you're being an idiot, Cass. For the first time in your life I think you are head over heels in love.' And with that comment she walked out the ward, leaving a shocked Cass still standing at the sink.

The rest of Cassidy's shift was bedlam. Every patient that was admitted was elderly and suffering from effects of the cold. It broke her heart.

'Is this the last one?' she asked as Brad appeared next to another patient being wheeled onto the ward.

He shook his head and ran his hand through his rumpled hair. 'Nope. I've just been paged by the doctor on-call service. They're sending another one in. Ten patients in the last twenty-four hours, all suffering from some effects of cold.' He shook his head in disbelief. 'You don't see this often in Australia. I think I've only ever looked after one case of hypothermia before. Today has been a huge learning curve.'

'Why so many?'

'The temperature apparently dropped to minus twenty last night. Some of these patients only get social-care services during the week—so some of them weren't discovered until this morning. The sad thing is, only two had heating systems that weren't working. The rest were just too scared to put them on because of the huge rise in their heating bills.'

Cassidy waited as they moved their patient over into the hospital bed. He was very frail, hardly any muscle tone at all, his skin hanging in folds around his thin frame. She bundled the covers around him. 'Go and see if you can find any spare duvets or blankets,' she asked one of the nursing auxiliaries.

Brad handed over his chart. 'Frank Johnson is eighty, lives alone and has a past history of COPD and heart disease. You can see he's underweight. He hasn't been eating, and when he was admitted his temperature was thirty-four degrees centigrade. He'd got so confused he'd actually started taking his clothes off, as he thought he was overheating. He was barely conscious when the social-care staff found him this morning.'

Cassidy nodded. It wasn't the first time she'd heard this. She looked at the IV fluids currently connected—often the patients admitted with hypothermia were also dehydrated. 'What's the plan for him?'

Brad pointed to the chart. 'He's been in A and E for a few hours, and his temperature is gradually climbing. It's thirty-six now, still below normal, but he's certainly less confused. Try and get some more fluids and some food into him. I want four-hourly obs and refer him to Social Services and Dietetics. We've got to try and get him some better assistance.' He waved his hand around the ward.

'In fact, those rules apply to just about everyone that's been admitted in the last twenty-four hours.' He looked down at his own bare arms, where his hairs were practically standing on end. 'It doesn't help that this place is freezing, too. What's going on?'

Cassidy gave him a weary smile. 'Old hospital, old heating system. This place is always like this in winter.'

'Tomorrow I'm going to bring in a sleeping bag and walk about in it. Do you think they'll get the hint and try to sort this place out?'

She laughed. 'That would be a sight to see. But good luck. Look at all the staff on the ward—all wearing two cardigans over their uniforms. I hate long sleeves—it's an infection-control hazard. But the temperature in this place is ridiculous. I can hardly tell them to take them off.'

'If you come into my office, I can think of an alternative way to heat you up.'

Cassidy's cheeks instantly flushed and she looked around to check no one had heard his comment. 'Brad!'

He gave her a wicked smile. 'We both know cold temperatures can cause confusion, and it wouldn't do for the doctors and nurses to be confused. I'm just trying to keep us at the top of our game.'

She titled her head to one side. 'Dr Donovan, if the cold is getting to you, I'll even go so far as to make you a cup of coffee. That should heat you up.'

'And if I'd prefer something else?'

'Then you'll just have to wait.' She folded her arms across her chest. It was almost time for the shift change—time to go home. And Brad must be due to finish as he'd been on call the night before. He looked knackered. As if he could keel over at any moment. But he could still manage to give her that sexy smile and those come-to-bed eyes. And no matter how much she told herself she should walk away, she just couldn't.

'I have something for you.'

'What?'

He pulled something from the pocket of his pale blue scrubs. A pair of rumpled tickets. Cassidy recognised the insignia on them instantly. Her mouth fell open. 'The skating rink! You remembered.'

'Of course I remembered. You said you wanted to go skating the night the ice rink opened in George Square so I bought us some tickets.'

She stared at the tickets. There it was again. Just when everything in her head was giving her lots of reasons to end this relationship.

Just when she hadn't been alone with him for a few days and felt as though she was starting to shake him out her system—he did something like this.

Something thoughtful. Something kind. Something that would matter only to her. He'd even managed to plan ahead—a trait distinctly lacking in most men she knew.

'So are we going to capture the spirit of Christmas?' he whispered in her ear.

One look from those big blue eyes and he was instantly back in her system. Like a double-shot espresso. 'You bet ya!' She smiled at him.

*20 November*

'I don't think we need an ice rink. These pavements are bad enough,' Brad grumbled as he grabbed hold of Cassidy's waist to stop her skidding one more time.

She slid her hand, encased in a red leather glove, into his. 'Don't be such a grump. And look at this place, it's buzzing! Isn't it great?'

Brad looked around. He had to admit Glasgow did the whole Christmas-decoration thing well. There were gold and red Christmas lights strung along the length of Buchanan Street, twinkling against the dark night sky, trying to keep the late-night shoppers in the mood for Christmas. The street was thronged with hundreds of people, all wrapped against the bitter-cold weather, their warm breath visible in the cold night air.

But even though the lights were impressive, he couldn't take his eyes off Cassidy. She seemed to have a coat for every colour of the rainbow. And in the last few days he had seen them all.

But it was her grandmother's red wool coat that suited her most, even though it probably wouldn't withstand the freezing temperatures of tonight.

This evening Cassidy had layered up with two cardigans beneath the slim-fitting coat. She had accessorised with a black hat and scarf and red leather gloves, with a pair of thick black boots on her feet. But even in all those clothes it was her eyes that sparkled most.

As they turned the corner into George Square, the lights were even brighter.

An international Christmas market filled the edges of the square, immediately swamping them in a delicious array of smells. The ice rink took up the middle of the square, with a huge Christmas tree—still to be lit—at one end and an observation wheel at the other.

Around the edges were an old-fashioned helter-skelter, a café/bar and a merry-go-round. Families were everywhere, children chattering with excitement about the lights being switched on.

For a second Brad felt something twisting around his heart. He wished more than anything that Melody could be here with him now. He'd never experienced Christmas in a cold climate, and he'd love it if his daughter could see this with him. He'd even seen an ad posted on the hospital notice-board the other day about a Santa's grotto with real, live reindeer down on the Ayrshire coast. If only he could take Melody to see something like that. The thought instantly clouded his head with difficult memories and yearnings.

He watched as a father lifted his daughter up onto one of the huge white horses with red reins on the merry-go-round. As the music started and the ride slowly began to move, he could see the father standing next to the horse, holding his daughter safely in place as her face glowed with excitement.

'Brad?'

He turned abruptly. Cassidy was watching him with her all-seeing, all-knowing brown eyes. She gave his arm a little tug. 'Are you okay?'

She followed his eyes to the merry-go-round, the question hesitating on her lips.

This wasn't the time to be melancholy. This was the time to be positive and thankful that he could create new memories with someone who tugged at his heartstrings. He reached out and grabbed her leather-gloved hand. 'Have I told you how beautiful you look tonight in your grandmother's coat? That red suits you perfectly.'

He pulled her forward for a kiss, ducking underneath the black furred hat that was currently containing her wayward curls. 'Do you remember those little girls who used to be on top of the chocolate boxes at Christmas? That's just what you look like.'

'Welcome, everyone.' The compère's voice echoed around the square and they turned to face him.

'Who is he?' Brad whispered.

'Some reality TV star,' she whispered back, 'but I've no idea which one.'

The guy was swamped in the biggest coat Brad had even seen. He obviously wasn't from around these parts. 'We're here in Glasgow tonight to light up our Christmas tree.'

There was a cheer around about them.

'Can anyone guess what colour the tree lights will be this year?'

He waited as the crowd shouted out around him. 'Let's count down and see. Altogether now, ten, nine, eight...'

Cassidy started to join in, shouting down the numbers with rest of the crowd. 'Come on, you.' She nudged him.

Brad smiled and started chanting with people around them. 'Five, four, three, two, *one*!'

There was a gasp as the tree lit up instantly with a whole host of red lights, like winter berries on the tree. A few seconds later they were joined by some tiny silver twinkling stars. A round of applause went up then, and only a few seconds later, Brad noticed Cassidy blink as a cheer erupted all around them. People were holding their hands out and laughing as the first smattering of snow appeared in tiny flakes around them. It only took a few seconds for some to land in the curls of her hair and on her cheeks. She gave a big smile, looking upwards to the dark sky. 'Nothing like a little dusting of snow for the occasion.'

Brad pulled his hand out of his thermal glove and held it out like the people around them. 'First time I've been snowed on,' he said, watching as the tiny flakes melted instantly as they touched his hand. 'This is fabulous.'

Cassidy sighed. 'Wait until the morning. If the snow lies on the roads and streets, it will be even more treacherous than before. In my experience snow generally means we'll be more busy at work.'

Brad grabbed her waist again. 'Work? Let's not talk about work. Let's go and have some fun.'

They walked around some of the nearby market stalls. Cassidy sampled some sautéed potatoes with onions and bacon then moved on to the next stall to try their vast array of chocolates. 'What's your favourite?' Brad asked. 'I'll buy you some.'

Cassidy's nose wrinkled and she glanced over her shoulder. 'Actually, I'm a tat collector. I'd prefer another ornament for my Christmas tree.'

He gave her a surprised look. 'A tree ornament instead of chocolate? I would never have guessed. Well, let's see what they've got.'

She was like a child in the proverbial sweetie shop as she oohed and aahed over tiny green sequin trees, little white angels and traditional wooden crafted Santa Claus ornaments. A few moments later Cassidy had selected a Russian doll for her tree with red and gold zigzags adorning its tiny wooden frame. 'This is perfect,' she said. 'I've never seen anything like this before.'

Brad smiled and handed over some money, but not before picking up a second one for Melody. She would have loved this stall, too.

They walked over to the nearby booth to collect their skates and spent a few minutes sitting at the side, lacing them up. Cassidy stood up, wobbling around as she tried to gain her balance. Brad appeared at her side, equally unsteady. 'Are we ready for this?' He held out his hand towards her.

They stepped onto the ice together. It was busy, families skating and wobbling with interlinked hands as they tried to find their way around the ice. Brad took a few moments to get his balance—he'd only ever skated a few times in his life but had always managed to stay upright. Cassidy, however, took him completely by surprise.

She let go of his hand and within seconds was gliding over the ice as if it was something she did every day. Her paces were long and even as she bobbed and weaved through the crowd of people on the ice. She spun round, her red coat swinging out around her. Brad held on to the side rail for a few more seconds.

'Come on, Dr Donovan, show us what

you're made of!' she shouted from the middle of the rink.

She looked gorgeous. Her cheeks were flushed with colour, and the red coat with its nipped-in waist highlighted her figure perfectly. The perfect Christmas picture.

Her words were like a challenge. And no matter how unsteady he was on the ice, Brad wasn't one to ignore a challenge. He pushed himself off as best he could towards her, nearly taking out a few children in the process. He reached her in a few seconds with only a few unsteady steps and wrapped his arms around her in the middle of the rink. 'You're a scammer, Cassidy Rae. You didn't say you knew how to ice skate.'

'You didn't ask.' Her eyes were twinkling as she pushed off and spun around him again, skating backwards for a few seconds before ending in an Olympic-style twirl.

'Show-off,' he growled. 'Where on earth did you learn how to do that?'

She started skating backwards around him. 'In Australia you surf—in Scotland you skate!' She reversed into him, allowing him to collapse his arms around her waist. 'That's not strictly true,' she said. 'I skated for around five years but, to be honest, as a young girl I was a bit flighty. I tried ballet, majorettes, country dancing and horse riding before I started skating.'

His head rested on her shoulder, his nose touching her pink flushed cheek. 'I like the sound of a flighty Cassidy Rae. She sounds like fun.'

Cassidy pushed off and turned to face him again, tilting her head to one side. 'Are you trying to say I'm not fun now, Dr Donovan?'

'Oh, you're lots of fun, Ms Rae.' He tried to take a grab at her, but his unsteady gait sent him wobbling across the ice. 'Help!'

She skated alongside him and slotted her hand into his. 'Let's just take things easy. We'll just skate around in a simple circle like the rest of the people are doing.' She pointed at some kids teetering past them. 'See? Anyone can do it.'

Brad groaned and tried to push more firmly on the ice. It was easier while Cassidy was gripping his hand, and he gained confidence as they circled round and round the rink. By the time the old-fashioned klaxon sounded, signalling the end of their session, Brad felt as though he could finally stand upright with some confidence.

'Is that an hour already? I can't believe it. I was finally starting to get the hang of this.'

'We can come back again,' said Cassidy

with a smile as she skated around him again. The rink was starting to empty as people crowded toward the small exit. He watched for a few seconds as Cassidy took advantage of the now-empty ice and did a few twirls. A squeal stopped her in her tracks.

Brad pushed through the throng, reaching a little girl who was being pulled up by her father and clutching her hand to her chest. Her face was pale and Brad could see a few drips of crimson blood on the ice at her feet.

'Let me have a look at her,' he said, lifting her up in his strong arms. 'I'm a doctor.' He turned his head towards Cassidy, who had appeared at his back. 'Can you ask the booth if they have a first-aid kit?'

The crowd parted easily, concerned by the cries of a child, and he walked unsteadily to the adjacent wooden bench at the side of the rink. He positioned the child underneath the nearest light and held her hand tightly for a few seconds.

'What's your name?' he asked the pale-faced, trembling little girl.

'Victoria,' she whispered. Brad smiled. It was clear she was trying very hard not to cry. Her father had his arms wrapped around her shoulders.

'She just fell over as we were waiting to

get off the ice. Someone must have caught her hand with their skate.'

Cassidy appeared with the first-aid kit and opened it quickly, pulling out some gloves, antiseptic wipes, sterile dressings and elastic bandages.

Brad got off the bench and lowered himself near the ground, his face parallel with Victoria's. 'I'm just going to have a little look at your hand—just for a second. Is that okay?'

She nodded but clutched her hand even closer to her chest.

He pulled off his gloves and held his hand at the side of her face. 'Can you feel how cold my fingers are?' He touched her cheek and she flinched a little, before smiling and nodding.

He picked up the gloves. 'I'm going to put these really funky blue gloves on before I have a little look. I might want to put a special bandage on your hand—is that okay?'

Victoria nodded, still looking tearful, but held her hand out tremulously to Brad.

Brad worked swiftly. He cleared her hand from her anorak sleeve and had a quick glance at the cut before stemming the flow of blood with a sterile pad. 'I'm going to give this a quick clean and bandage it up for you.'

He nodded at Cassidy as she ripped open the antiseptic wipes for him.

'Ouch!' squealed Victoria, as the wipe lightly touched her skin.

'All done,' said Brad almost simultaneously. He took one more look now that the blood was clear, then applied another sterile non-adherent pad and elastic bandage to put a little pressure on the wound. He looked at Cassidy. 'Which hospital is nearest to here?'

'The Royal Infirmary,' she answered. 'Less than five minutes in a taxi.'

Brad gave the anxious father a smile. 'I'm afraid she's going to need some stitches and the wound cleaned properly. The pad shouldn't stick to her skin and the elastic bandage gives a little pressure to stem the flow of blood before you get to the hospital. But it's not a long-term solution. Are you able to take her up to the A and E unit?'

The father nodded. He pulled a phone from his pocket and started pressing buttons. 'I have a friend who's a taxi driver in the city centre. He'll come and get us.'

Brad leaned forward and whispered in Victoria's ear. 'You're a very brave girl. And do you know what brave girls get?' He reached into his pocket and pulled out his little Russian doll. It was almost identical to the one he'd just bought for Cassidy, but this one had silver and pink zigzags and a long silver string to hang it from the tree.

'This is a special Christmas-tree decoration—just for you.'

Victoria's eyes lit up, his distraction technique working like a charm. Cassidy's felt a lump at the back of her throat that she tried to swallow. He must have bought an extra ornament when he'd paid for hers earlier. And it didn't take much imagination to know who he'd bought it for.

There it was.

Right in front of her, glowing like a beacon. All the reasons why Brad shouldn't be without his daughter. She gathered up the remnants of the first-aid kit, stuffing them back inside, and disappeared back to the booth.

She couldn't watch that. She couldn't watch him interact with a child in such an easy and relaxed manner. It showed what she already knew deep down but hadn't wanted to admit.

Brad was good with kids. No, Brad was *great* with kids. He knew just when to act and what to say. He deserved to have kids. He deserved to be with his daughter. He deserved to know where she was and play a part in her life.

And even though he hadn't said much

around her over the last few days, it was clear that Melody was in the forefront of his mind.

She felt ashamed. Ashamed of the words she'd uttered and the thoughts she'd had while she'd been talking to Lucy. Thoughts that he might be willing to forget about his daughter and just have a life with her. What kind of person was she?

She'd seen the haunted look in his eyes earlier when he'd been watching the father and daughter on the merry-go-round. But she hadn't been able to say the words—to ask him if he was hurting and what she could do to help.

She looked over at him now, and he gave her a wave as he walked with Victoria and her father to a black cab parked at the side of the square. Her hand lifted automatically in response, but it was the expression on his face that was killing her.

She'd never seen Brad look so comfortable and so at ease.

She knew what he needed more than anything. He needed to find his daughter.

# CHAPTER SEVEN

*29 November*

'Hi, Cassidy, nice to see you.'

'Hi, Grace, how's Gran today?'

The nurse walked around the desk and joined Cassidy. 'She's in here today,' she said as she walked into a large sitting room looking out over well-tended gardens. 'She's been really confused these last few days, but unusually quiet, too.'

'Is she eating okay?'

Grace nodded. 'She's eating well. She seems quite focused when she gets her meals. But as soon as she's finished, she's off wandering.' She walked over and touched Cassidy's gran on her shoulder. 'Tillie, your granddaughter is here to see you again.'

Cassidy's heart fell as her gran barely even looked up, her eyes still fixed on the garden. She gave Grace a half-hearted smile. 'Thank you, Grace.'

'No problem. Give me a shout if you need anything.'

Cassidy sat down in the chair opposite her gran. Her heart was fluttering in her chest. She was wearing her gran's red wool coat and she wondered if she would notice. She pulled off her leather gloves and reached over and took her gran's hand.

'Hi, Gran.' She brushed a kiss on her cheek.

Tillie looked at her only for a second, her confusion immediately evident. She didn't recognise Cassidy.

Cassidy took a deep breath. It had been like this for the last few months. The little spells of recognition and memory were becoming fewer and fewer. She'd had some episodes where she'd mistaken Cassidy for her mother, but it had been over a year since she'd recognised Cassidy for herself.

This was the part that broke her heart. Her gran had always been her confidante, her go-to person. The person who gave her the best advice in the world—something she badly needed right now.

She opened her bag and stared at the pile of envelopes inside. They'd revealed more than she wanted to know. But it was the photograph that haunted her most. Her gran had always been warm and caring towards her. But she couldn't remember ever seeing her gran like she was in that photograph—her eyes filled with adoration for the man standing by her side. Her whole face glowing with happiness. Had she really known her gran at all?

'I've been at the house, Gran. Everything's fine.' Her fingers caught the edge of the collar of her coat and she bit her lip nervously. 'I found this beautiful coat in the one of the cupboards. It was wrapped up with some letters.' She pulled the bundle from her bag, But Tillie's eyes were still fixed on the garden. Cassidy swallowed, trying to get rid of the lump in her throat.

The garden was covered in frost and a light dusting of snow, but the beds in front of the window brimmed with life. They were filled with evergreen bushes with red berries, coloured heather plants and deep pink pernettya plants. The planters around the edges had an eruption of coloured cyclamen and white heathers. It was beautiful.

Cassidy looked out over the horizon. Everything about this spelled Christmas to her. She wondered what plants they had in Australia at this time of year. Would there be anything as nice as this? How could anyone feel festive in a baking-hot climate?

She'd thought about that often over the last

few days, the thoughts just drifting into her mind when she least expected them. She'd had numerous friends who'd emigrated and they all raved about it, saying it had been the best move of their lives. They sent her pictures of spending Christmas Day on the beach, cooking on the barbeque or having dinner in the sunshine next to the pool.

But Christmas always meant cold weather, frost and snow to Cassidy. She just couldn't imagine it any other way. Could she really feel festive in a bikini?

'Hello, dear. Who are you?'

Cassidy flinched and pushed the thoughts from her mind as her gran spoke to her, her eyes suddenly bright with life.

'I'm Cassidy, your granddaughter. I've come for a visit, Gran.'

'How lovely. Do you have any tea?'

Cassidy smiled. Her gran was a true tea genie and could drink twenty cups a day. She slid her hand into her gran's. 'I've come to tell you that I've met a nice man, Gran. One who's making me think about a lot of things.'

Tillie nodded but didn't say anything. Cassidy took a deep breath. 'When I found your coat, I also found a parcel of letters.' She hesitated for a second. 'I hope you don't mind, but I read them, Gran. The ones from Peter Johnson, your US Air Force friend.'

She paused, waiting to see if would get any reaction. She knew some people would think she was strange, trying to have a normal conversation with a confused old lady, but to Cassidy she couldn't communicate any other way. She loved and respected her gran, and she hoped beyond hope that some of what she said might get through. 'He looked lovely, Gran.'

She pulled out the black-and-white photograph. 'I found a picture of you—you look so happy.' She couldn't help the forlorn sound to her voice as she handed the photo to her gran.

Tillie took it in her frail fingers and touched the surface of the photograph. 'So pretty,' she murmured, before handing it back.

Cassidy sat backwards in her chair. 'He wrote you some lovely letters. You never told me about him—I wish you had.' She stared out the windows, lost in thought.

She'd read the letters the night before, tears rolling down her face. Peter Johnson had met her gran while he'd been stationed in Prestwick with the US Army Air Force. His letters were full of young love and hope for the future. Filled with promises of a life in the

US. Most had come from Prestwick, with a few from Indiana at a later date.

Had he been her gran's first love? What had happened to him? Had he gone back to the US and forgotten about her? Her gran could have had the chance of another life, on another continent. Had she wanted to go to the US? What had stopped her? Had she suffered from any of the doubts and confusion that she herself was feeling right now?

She looked back at her gran, who was running her fingers over the sleeve of her coat. 'I wish you could tell me, Gran.' Tears were threatening to spill down her cheeks. 'I really need some advice. I need you to tell me what I should do.'

'What a lovely colour,' her gran said suddenly, before sitting back in her chair. 'Did you bring tea?' she asked.

Cassidy gave Tillie's hand a squeeze. 'I'll go and get you some tea, Gran,' she said, standing up and heading over to the kitchen. She'd been here often enough to know where everything was kept.

The girl in the kitchen gave her a nod and handed over a teapot and two cups. She glanced at her watch. 'I thought it was about that time for your gran. I was just about to bring this over.' She smiled as Cassidy lifted up the tray, before reaching over and touching the shoulder of her coat. 'What a beautiful coat, Cassidy. It's a really nice style. It suits you.'

Cassidy blushed. 'Thank you. I found it the other day.' She nodded over her shoulder. 'It was Gran's.'

'Really? I'm surprised. It looks brand new.' She raised her eyebrows. 'I bet she cut up a storm in that coat a few years ago.'

Cassidy's felt her shoulders sag. 'I don't know, Karen. Truth is, I never saw my gran wear this coat. But I found a picture of her in it and she looked amazing.'

'I bet she did.' Karen gave her a smile. 'You know, Cassidy, I know it's hard seeing your gran like this, but you've got to remember that she's happy here. Although she's frail, her physical health is good for someone her age and most days she seems really content.'

Cassidy nodded gratefully. 'I know, Karen.' She looked over to where her gran was sitting, staring out the window again. 'I just wish I could have the old her back sometimes—even for just a few minutes.'

Karen gave her arm a squeeze. 'I know, honey.'

Cassidy carried the tea tray over and waited a few minutes before pouring a cup for her gran. She was fussy about her tea—not too weak, not too strong, with just the right amount of milk.

Cassidy kept chatting as she sat next to her. It didn't matter to her that her gran didn't understand or acknowledge what she was saying. It felt better just telling her things. In the last year she'd found that just knowing she'd told her gran something could make her feel a million times better—sometimes even help her work things out in her head.

'I've met a nice Australian man. He's a doctor who's working with me right now.' Her gran nodded and smiled. Often it seemed as if she liked to hear the music and tone of Cassidy's voice. 'The only thing is, he has a little girl who is missing right now. He really wants to find her. And when he does...' she took a deep breath '...he'll go.'

The words sounded so painful when she said them out loud.

And for a second they stopped her in her tracks.

What would she do if Brad just upped and disappeared? How would she feel if she could never see him again?

It didn't take long for the little part of her she didn't like to creep into her brain again. Chances were Melody might never be found.

Brad might decide to stay in Scotland for a while longer.

She felt a wave of heat wash over her like a comfort blanket. That would be perfect. Maybe she could consider a trip to Australia? That wouldn't be so hard. It was a beautiful country and it might even be interesting to see the differences in nursing in another country.

She looked outside at the frosty weather. Her gran had started singing under her breath. A sweet lullaby that she used to sing to Cassidy as a child. Memories came flooding back, of dark nights in front of the fire cuddled up on Gran's couch.

Part of the issue for Cassidy was that she loved the Scottish winters and cold weather. As a pale-skinned Scot, she'd never been a fan of the blazing-hot sunshine. And even when she'd gone on holiday, she hadn't lain beside the pool for a fortnight; she'd needed to be up and about doing things.

Most people she knew would love the opportunity to live in a warmer climate but Cassidy had never even considered it. Not for a second.

Could she really start to consider something like that now?

Everything was making her head spin. Her

relationship with Brad was becoming serious. She really needed to sit down and talk to him again.

She looked at her gran, who was sipping her tea delicately, trying to hear the words she thought her gran might say in her head.

She could imagine the elderly lady telling her not to be so pathetic. To make up her mind about what she wanted and to go get it. She could also sense the old-fashioned disapproval her gran might have about the fact Brad had a child with someone else. A child he wasn't being allowed to fulfil his parental duties towards. Her gran would certainly have had something to say about that.

But would she have been suspicious like some of Brad's colleagues in Australia? Or would she have been sympathetic towards him?

Cassidy just wasn't sure. And finding the letters and photographs made her even less sure. She'd thought she'd known everything about her gran. Turned out she hadn't. And now she'd no way of picking up those lost strands of her life.

She heaved a sigh and looked out over the garden again. She was going to have to sort this out for herself.

## 30 November

Brad came rushing into the restaurant ten minutes late, with his tie skewed to one side and his top button still undone. 'I'm so sorry,' he gasped as he sat down opposite her. 'There was a last-minute admission just before I left, and Luca was at a cardiac arrest so I couldn't leave.'

Cassidy gave him a smile and lifted her glass of wine towards him. 'No worries, Brad, I started without you.'

He reached over and pulled the bottle of wine from the cooler at the side of the table and filled his glass. She leaned across the table. 'Here, let me,' she said as her deft fingers did up his top button and straightened his tie.

She didn't care that he'd been late. His conscientiousness at work was one of the reasons she liked him so much.

He raised his glass to her. 'Cheers.' The glasses clinked together and Cassidy relaxed back into her chair.

Brad ducked under the table. 'Here, I bought you something.' He handed a plastic bag over to Cassidy.

She raised her eyebrows. 'Did you wrap it yourself?' she quipped.

'Ha, ha. Just look and see what it is.'

Cassidy peeked inside the plastic bag and gingerly put her hand inside—all she could see was a mixture of red and green felt. She pulled out her present and felt a mixture of surprise and a tiny bit of disappointment. It was an advent calendar, the fabric kind with pockets for each of the twenty-four days. The kind she'd told Brad she didn't like.

She looked over at him and he gave her a beaming smile. 'I thought in the spirit of making some nice Christmas memories I would try and convert you.'

She wrinkled her nose. 'Convert me? Why?'

He shrugged. 'You like the paper-type advent calendar. I always had one of these in Australia that my mum made for me. She used to put something in the pockets for only a few days at a time because she knew I would have looked ahead otherwise.' He touched the first few pockets and she heard a rustling sound. 'And they're *not* all chocolates.'

She nodded and gave him a smile. 'So, you're trying to convert me, are you? Well, I'm willing to give it a go. But how do you plan on filling up the other pockets?'

There it was. That little twinkle in his eye

as he took a sip of his wine. 'That's the thing. If you want your calendar filled, you'll have to keep letting me into your flat. In fact, I'll need unlimited access.'

She loved the way his smile stretched from ear to ear. The restaurant was dim, with subdued lighting and flickering candlelight. His eyes seemed even bluer than normal, their colour amplified as they reflected off his pale blue shirt.

'Did you plan this just so you could get into my flat?'

He shook his head, his face becoming a little more serious. 'I just think you've been a little quiet these past few days. As if something was on your mind.' His fingers reached across the table and intertwined with hers. 'I'm just trying to find a way to stay in your life.'

She felt shocked by the openness and honesty of his words. She kept her gaze stuck on the advent calendar as she tried to think of what to say. Things had been a little unsettled between them.

'I'm just a little unsure of what's happening between us,' she started slowly. She lifted her eyes. 'I like you, Brad.'

'And I like you, too, Cassidy. You know that.'

He wasn't making this any easier. It was hard enough, trying to get the words out. His fingers were tracing little circles on the palm of her hand. Just like he did after they'd made love together.

'I'm just worried that I'm getting in too deep and before we know it you'll be gone.'

His brow creased. 'Why would you think that?'

She pulled her hand away from his. It was too distracting. 'I don't know. I just think that I'm from Scotland, you're from Australia...' She threw her hands up in frustration, then levelled her gaze at him. 'I know you don't want to stay here and I don't want to move away. So where does that leave us?'

She could feel tears nestling behind her eyes. That was the last thing she wanted to happen. She didn't want to cry.

Her mind was flooded with thoughts of her gran. Truth was, she would never find out what happened between her gran and Peter Johnson. Maybe it had only been a wartime fling, with no substance behind it. Or maybe her gran had given up the chance of a lifetime to go and live abroad with the man who'd made her face sparkle.

What Cassidy would never know was whether her gran regretted her decisions. If she could go back, would she do something different?

Was *she* about to make the same mistake?

Brad reached back over and took her hand again. 'Cassidy, I have no idea what's going to happen. All I know is I love spending time with you and I don't want it to end. I've no idea what will happen in the next few years— I've been offered an extension to my job here for another six months, and I've decided to take it. You know I'm not going to stop looking for my daughter. Is that what this is all about? Melody?'

Cassidy shook her head. 'No, it's not about Melody.' Then she hesitated. 'But I don't know what to think about all that. At the end of the day, Brad, we could continue to have a relationship for the next few months and then you could get a call one day about Melody and just disappear. I don't think I could handle that.'

And there it was, staring him in the face. All the while he was practically telling her she was bullheaded and stubborn, her biggest vulnerability lay on the table between them. Abandonment.

He'd sensed it in her for a while. When she'd mentioned her ex-fiancé, her parents or her ill grandmother. That fear of being alone.

He shook his head, the expression on his face pained. 'Remember, Cassidy, I've been on the other side of this fence. I've had someone disappear out of my life with no warning. And I know how much it hurts. I would never do that to another human being.'

She could tell her words had stung, and she hadn't meant them to. It was just so difficult to describe the mishmash of emotions in her head. Even she couldn't understand them, so how could she expect Brad to?

The waiter appeared at their side with some menus, and Cassidy pulled her hand from Brad's to take one. Her eyes ran up and down the menu quickly before Brad lifted it from her hands.

'Don't tell me, you'll have the mushrooms and the chicken.'

Cassidy groaned. 'Don't tell me I'm that predictable.' She grabbed the menu back and ran her eyes along the text again with a sinking realisation that Brad was right. She *did* always have the mushrooms and the chicken. The only time she ever deviated was if neither was on the menu.

He leaned forward, giving her that smile again. 'Why don't you surprise us both and pick something totally different? In fact, close your eyes and just point at something and order that.'

Cassidy shivered. 'Yuck.' Even the thought of doing that was too much for her. Imagine if she ended up with something she didn't like—or never ate? That would be hideous. 'I can't do that, Brad, I might get seaweed or fillet steak.'

His eyes gleamed as he did a pretend shudder. 'Mmm, and that would be awful, wouldn't it? Take this as a test, Cassidy.'

'A test for what?'

He folded his napkin in his lap, as if he was choosing his words carefully. 'For a thoroughly modern woman, you can be pretty closed-minded about some things.'

An uncomfortable feeling crept down her spine. 'What do you mean?'

'You can have some pretty fixed ideas.'

Cassidy shook her head. 'I just know my own mind. There's nothing wrong with that.'

He paused. 'I didn't say there was. But sometimes you make your mind up about things without looking at the whole picture.'

Cassidy was feeling rattled now and a little irritated. So much for a romantic dinner. 'What do you mean exactly?'

He licked his lips and she saw him take a deep breath. There was something different in his eyes. The normal laid-back look was gone. 'What I mean, Cassidy, is that you've written me—and others—off with no thought or regard for our feelings, just because we live in a different country. Now, if you'd been abroad and stayed there for a while and didn't enjoy it, it might seem a reasonable conclusion to have come to. But you haven't. You've never done it. You've never even tried. And what's more—you won't even consider it.'

He looked frustrated by her, angry even, and she felt a tight feeling spread across her chest. Not even Bobby, her Spanish fiancé, had called her like this. She'd just refused to go with him and that had been that. He hadn't questioned her reasoning behind her decision. He hadn't made *her* question her reasoning behind the decision.

But Brad hadn't finished. He was on a roll. 'It's the same with your menu choices and your Christmas traditions.' He leaned over and picked up the advent calendar. 'You say you only like the picture calendars but you've never even tried one of these, have you?' She saw his shoulders sag, tension easing out of them, and the tone of his voice altered.

'All I'm trying to do is get you to look outside your box. To look at the world that surrounds you and open your mind to other ideas, other experiences, other…' he paused before ending '…possibilities.'

He was holding his breath, waiting to see what she would say. She should stop, she should think and ponder what he was saying to her and why. But Cassidy went with her first instinct. She was mad.

She flung her napkin on the table. 'So why are you bothering with me, Brad? You don't date someone with the idea of changing them. You date someone because you like them the way they are, not the way *you* want them to be.' She spat the words at him.

'I'm not trying to change you. I like you, everything about you. But if we have any hope of a future together, you're going to have to learn to bend a little.'

'Meaning what?'

'Meaning that I would love to promise to stay with you in Scotland for the next thirty years, but what if I do get that call about my daughter? What if I do need to go to the States? That's it for us? Just like that—because you won't even consider any other possibility?'

He made it all sound so unreasonable. So closed-minded. But inside she didn't feel like that.

'Or what if I get a great opportunity to

work in another country? You won't even consider coming with me? Because you can't leave Scotland?'

'But my gran, I can't leave my gran.' It was the first thing that sprang to mind. The first brick in her feeble wall of defence.

Brad shook his head. 'I'm not asking you to leave your gran, Cassidy. Even though you know she's somewhere she's been taken care of. I'm just trying to see if you'll at least *consider* the possibility.'

Silence hung in the air between them. Her temper had dissipated as quickly as it had arisen.

He was making sense. Inside she knew he was making sense. But to admit it made her seem so petty.

The waiter appeared at their side again. 'Are you ready to order?'

Cassidy didn't even glance at the menu, she just thrust it back at the waiter. 'I'll have the chilli prawns and the Cajun salmon,' she said as she looked Brad square in the eye.

She could see the pulse at the side of his neck flickering furiously. How long had he been holding all this in? Chances were he'd been waiting to say this to her for the last few weeks. And he was right.

Although there was no way she was going to admit it right now.

Tiny little thoughts of Australia had started to penetrate her brain. Little sparks, curiosity and wonder had been creeping in over the last few weeks. Would she like it there? What would it be like to be in a different country for more than a two-week holiday?

It wasn't as if she'd never left the sunny shores of Scotland. She'd been all over the world—Spain, Italy, the US, even the Bahamas. But only for two weeks at a time. And by the time the plane had hit the tarmac back at Glasgow Airport, she'd always been glad to get back home.

But she had lots of friends who'd gone to other countries to work. The most popular place lately had been Dubai. Five of the nurses she'd worked with in Glasgow City Hospital had all upped sticks and gone to work there. All of them loved it and most had no intention of coming back to Glasgow. Two other members of staff had gone to work for aid organisations—one to Africa and one to Médecins Sans Frontières.

Why was she so different? Why had she never wanted to go and work somewhere else? Why did she feel as if her roots were firmly planted in Scottish soil?

Brad lifted the wine bottle and topped up her glass. She hadn't even heard what he'd ordered. She only hoped it was chicken so she could swap her salmon for it.

He lifted his glass to her. 'So, what do you say, Cassidy? Can we raise a toast to trying new things?'

She swallowed hard, her fingers brushing the tiny pockets of the advent calendar on the table in front of her. This couldn't be too hard. She could try this, couldn't she?

He was staring across the table at her, with those big blue eyes, tanned skin and perfect smile. Everything about him made her stomach still lurch. She'd never felt like this before. Could she honestly just walk away?

This had to be worth fighting for.

# CHAPTER EIGHT

*4 December*

CASSIDY woke up with a smile on her face. She glanced at the calendar hanging on her wall. Maybe embracing new change wasn't such a bad thing.

Brad's gifts had proved personal and thoughtful. She'd found an orange Belgian chocolate in the first pocket—one that she'd remarked on that night at the George Square market. For once she hadn't been instantly offended by the thought of a chocolate-filled calendar.

Next had been a tiny green sequin Christmas tree complete with red string, and in the third pocket she'd found a sprig of mistletoe.

It only took her seconds to push her feet into her red slippers and wrap her dressing gown around her shoulders. Brad had been on call again last night, so she hadn't seen him.

Her brow wrinkled. Pocket number four looked distinctly flat—maybe he hadn't had time to put something in there yet? She flicked the switch on the kettle and pulled a cup from the cupboard, before finally touching the pocket. There was a faint rustling noise. She pulled a piece of paper from the pocket and unfolded it.

It said, *'Look under the tree—not everything can fit in these tiny pockets!'*

She left the kettle boiling and walked through to her living room. There, under the tree he'd helped her decorate a few days before, was a red, glistening parcel. She couldn't wipe the smile from her face as she unwrapped the paper. It was a book. But not just any book. It was the latest thriller from her favourite Glasgow author—one she'd been meaning to buy herself.

Cassidy sagged back against the cushions on her sofa. Yet another thoughtful gift. One that meant something to her. Picked up from a chance conversation they'd had in the middle of the night on one shift.

She looked out at the overcast sky. It was going to be another miserable day. Time to wrap up warmly and head up the frosty hill to the hospital. She heard a noise at her door—a key turning in the lock and a whoosh of cold air blasting across the room.

'Brad, what are you doing here?'

Brad was barely recognisable among the layers of clothing he was wearing. All she could really see clearly were his blue eyes peering out from the balaclava-type head-wear he'd started wearing to protect himself from the cold. He was brandishing some cups. 'A skinny caramel latte for my favourite woman.'

She smiled. 'I'd hug you, but you're too cold.'

He sat down next to her, hands clenched around his cup. 'I'd take off my jacket but let me heat up first. It's Baltic out there.'

She laughed. 'So, you're finally connecting with our language. That's something I would normally say—not you.'

He nudged her. 'You must be rubbing off on me.' He bent over, his cold nose brushing against her, and she let out a squeal.

'Get away, ice man!' He wrapped his arms around her, trapping her on the sofa.

'This is an emergency. I need some body heat. I can't take these cold winters!'

She pretended to squirm as he held her tight. 'Drink your coffee. That will heat you up.'

'I can think of a better way to heat up,' he

whispered as he grabbed her hand and led her back through to her warm bed.

*10 December*

Today she had a magic wand. Pocket ten had held another little note that had led her to find it wrapped in silver paper, balanced on the branches of the tree.

He'd asked her favourite film character the other night and she'd declared she'd always wanted to be Glinda, the good witch of the north, from *The Wizard of Oz*. So he'd bought her a magic wand. And right now she really wanted to wave it above her medical receiving unit.

In the last twenty-four hours every single one of the thirty beds in the unit had been emptied and refilled. Patients were never supposed to stay in the medical receiving unit. Patients were supposed to be assessed and transferred to one of the other wards, but the current rate of transfer was ridiculous, for both the staff and the patients.

She replaced the phone receiver. Her staff was run ragged. The bed manager was getting snarky—she had patients in A and E waiting to be admitted. The normally pristine ward looked chaotic. There were a few random patient belonging bags sitting at the nurses' station, obviously misplaced or forgotten in the preceding few hours. And as for the ward clerk—she'd disappeared in tears five minutes ago.

Cassidy took a deep breath. This was the story of Scottish hospitals in the middle of an icy winter. It was only eight o'clock in the morning. She had to take control of this situation. Something was going to give. And she didn't want it to be her—or her staff.

She lifted her hands above her head. 'Everyone, stop!'

For a second there was silence. Cassidy never raised her voice on the ward and her staff looked startled. A few heads stuck out from doors down the corridor.

'Everyone…' she gestured her hands towards the desk '…come here. This will take five minutes.'

Her bewildered staff walked towards the nursing station. Some were carrying electronic nursing notes, some bed linen and towels.

Cassidy waited until they'd all assembled. One of the phlebotomists and ECG technicians appeared, too. She took another deep breath.

'Everyone, let's calm down. I want you all

to take a deep breath and tell me calmly what help you need.' She laid one hand on the desk. 'I can tell you that right now, no matter what the bed manager says, we will not move another patient until after lunchtime today. We need time to assess these patients properly.'

She gestured to the bags on the floor. 'We need to make sure that patients' belongings don't go astray.' She lowered her voice. 'More importantly, I need my team to know that they do a good job.'

She could see the visible calm descending on the ward as the rumble of the meal trolley could be heard approaching. 'What about the patients in A and E?' asked one of the younger staff nurses.

Cassidy shook her head. 'A and E is full of competent nursing staff. They are more than capable of starting the assessments for their patients. I'm going to phone them now and tell them to arrange breakfast and lunch for those patients. They won't be moving any more up here until after lunchtime.'

A number of shoulders relaxed around her. 'What about the bed manager?'

Cassidy smiled. 'Let me deal with her. Now...' she looked over at the staff surrounding her '...Fiona and Claire, go for your tea break. Michael...' she nodded to the tall, dark-haired nurse beside her '…you start the drug round. Linda and Ann, you help Joanne, the domestic, with the breakfasts.' The two auxiliaries scurried off, glad to have a simple task to perform.

Cassidy noticed Janice, the ward clerk, sniffing at her side. 'What's wrong, Janice?'

'It's the off-duty. It was supposed to be in for yesterday. But there's still a few shifts that need to be covered.'

Cassidy's eyes swept over the blank spaces in the book. Her brain shifted into gear. One of her senior staff nurses had asked if she could start taking over the off-duty rota. And she'd made an absolute mess of it, something Cassidy would have to deal with at a later date.

Just what she would have expected. One short for the night shift on Christmas Eve. The same thing happened every year without fail.

Her mind drifted back to the night at smelly-cat-woman's house. She almost cringed as she remembered she'd offered to do the night shift if she was a Christmas bride.

She could almost laugh out loud. Although the thought didn't seem anything like as ridiculous as it had before.

Things between her and Brad were good—
better than good. Her brain had started to ra-
tionalise things for her. Australia was one day
away. All twenty-four hours of one day, but
still only one day away from Scotland.

The more stories he told her about his life
there, the more curious she became. But
something else was becoming clearer to her.
Just like it had when Brad had naturally came
home to her flat the other day after his shift
had finished.

She wanted to see him all the time. She
wanted to be with him all the time. If he was
on call and she didn't see him one day, she
missed him. Something that had hit her like
a bolt out of the blue.

Cassidy had spent the last two years living life on her own. Her gran's memory had
deteriorated to the point she didn't recognise
Cassidy, and it had left her feeling even more
alone than before. She rarely heard from her
parents. But all of sudden it felt as if she had
family again.

And having Brad around just felt so *right*.

She didn't expect to be a Christmas bride,
but she did expect to have Brad in her future.

She pointed. 'Swap these two around.
Lorna prefers her night shifts together. And

I'll cover the night shift on Christmas Eve. Okay?'

'Are you sure?' The clerk was looking at her through red-rimmed eyes.

She gave her shoulder a squeeze. 'Yes, I'm sure. Now, just send it in and go make yourself a cup of tea.'

She went through to her office and made an uncomfortable call to the bed manager then walked quickly through the ward, helping the auxiliaries sit some patients up in bed for breakfast and helping another few patients into chairs. Luca appeared at her side and started reviewing some of the patients who had been admitted overnight. He gave her a smile. 'I hear you're leading a revolt up here this morning.'

She nodded. 'Happy to join in?'

'Absolutely. I feel as if I hardly got to see some of these patients in A and E.'

'It was the same for my staff. We weren't getting the chance to assess the patients properly before we sent them on.' She looked up and down the length of the ward, which seemed much calmer. 'I'm not allowing that to happen. We have a duty of care to these patients and I won't compromise.'

'Tell that to the bed manager.'

'I just did.' She shrugged her shoulders.

'Although she hates me right now, first and foremost she is a nurse, so she does understand the issues.'

The phone started ringing again, and since she'd sent the ward clerk off for tea, Cassidy leaned forward and picked it up. 'Medical receiving unit, Sister Rae speaking. Can I help you?'

The words she heard chilled her to the bone, and she gestured frantically to Luca for a piece of paper and then started scribbling furiously.

'What's wrong?' he asked as she replaced the phone.

'It's my grandmother. She's had a fall at the nursing home—they think she might have broken her hip.' She started to look around about her, searching for her bag. 'I need to go. They've taken her to another hospital at the other side of the city.'

Luca stood up. 'What can I do?'

Cassidy started pulling on the cardigan that was draped over her chair. She couldn't think straight. She couldn't think at all. The rational parts of her brain had stopped working. Gran was in her eighties and had chest problems. How often did an elderly person have problems with the anaesthetic? What if this was the last time she'd ever see her gran again?

She started to pace up the corridor. 'Michael, are you there?'

His head ducked out from behind a set of curtains.

'I'm really sorry but I need to go. It's an emergency—my gran. They think she might have broken her hip.'

'Of course, Cassidy. No problem.'

'You've got the keys to the drug trolley, haven't you? Here's the controlled-drug key.' She unpinned it from inside her uniform pocket. 'Can you let Lucy, Sister Burns from next door, know that I've had to leave?' She was babbling and she knew it.

'Cassidy, we'll be fine. I'll get some help from next door if we need it. And I won't start transferring any patients until after lunch.' He gave her a quick hug, then placed a hand firmly at her back. 'Now, go.'


His pager sounded again, and Brad growled and rolled over. 'I'm sleeping. I'm not on call any more. Leave me alone,' he groaned.

But the pager wasn't listening. It sounded again. And again. And again.

Brad was mad. Last night had been ridiculous. He hadn't stopped—not even for a minute. And on the way to work last night his Mini had made the strangest sound then phutted to a stop at the side of the road. And all he wanted to do this morning was lie in his bed and vegetate.

He flung back the covers, squinting at the light coming through the blinds, and lifted the pager to his scrunched-up eyes.

*'Call Joe immediately.'*

All of a sudden he was wide awake, his heart thumping in his chest. Joe Scott was his very expensive, US private investigator. He emailed Brad every few weeks, telling him any leads he was following and how he was getting on.

They had an understanding. Joe knew that Brad was a doctor, frequently on call, and had agreed that Joe would only contact Brad via his pager if something significant turned up. It had seemed the easiest solution as messages to a busy hospital could be lost, and depending on his rota sometimes Brad could be away from his house and normal emails for a few days at a time.

He reached for his phone, pushing in the number that was ingrained there.

'Joe, it's Brad Donovan. What have you found?'

'Haven't you read the email I sent you? I sent you some photographs.'

It took a few seconds for Brad's ears to adjust to the American accent. Email. He hadn't looked at his emails for two days.

He moved automatically to his laptop, his bare feet padding across the floor. It took for ever to boot up.

'I'm just opening the email now, Joe,' he said. 'Give me a few minutes.' He wasn't sure what was waking him up more quickly—the shock phone call or the cold air.

The email took for ever to open. He could sense Joe waiting impatiently at the other end of the phone. He didn't even read the content, just clicked on one of the attached photographs.

There she was. Blonde ringlets framing her face, dressed in a green puffy coat, throwing back her head and laughing. It was a beautiful sight.

'Is it her?' The US voice cut into his thoughts.

For a moment he couldn't speak. She'd grown so much. She looked like a proper little girl now—a little lady even, rather than a toddler. His eyes swept the surrounding area. Alison was standing in the background, holding a baby. She was laughing, too. Melody was positioned on the pebbled shoreline of a lake and was clutching stones in her hands.

He tried not to let the rage overwhelm him. He couldn't let that get in the way right now.

This was the first time he'd laid eyes on his little girl in nearly two years.

'Brad? Are you there?' The voice was strained now, obviously worried by his lack of response.

'Yes,' he croaked. 'It's Melody.' There was an unfamiliar sensation overwhelming him right now. It was a mixture of relief, joy, bitterness and excitement.

'Great. I was sure I'd found them, but needed you to confirm it.'

Brad's mind started to race. His eyes couldn't move from the photograph. They looked to be out in the middle of nowhere.

'Where are they?'

'North Woods, Wisconsin. Lots of hills and dense woods, terrible phone and internet reception. Took the photo two days ago. You were right about Alison, she got married. Her name is now Alison Johnson. Married to Blane Johnson—a paediatrician in Wisconsin—and they have a baby daughter, Temperance.'

Brad could tell he was reading from the notes in front of him. But he didn't care. He still couldn't believe it. And the picture was crystal clear. Not some blurry snap, which he might have expected. He could almost reach out and touch her. Did she remember him?

Did she remember she had a dad who loved her very much?

His fingers brushed the screen. She looked happy. She looked healthy. Part of him gave a little sigh of relief. His daughter was alive, happy and healthy. For any parent, that should be the most important thing.

He was trying so hard to keep a lid on his feelings. He'd spent the last two years thinking about what he'd do when he found her. Thoughts of taking his time and trying to contact Alison separately, engaging a lawyer, getting advice on his legal rights in another country, finding out about extradition from that particular state in the US. And now all those rational, sensible thoughts were flying out the window.

Something registered in his brain—geography had never been his strong point. 'Where is it? Where's North Woods, Wisconsin?'

He heard Joe let out a guffaw. 'I thought you might ask that. Not the most straightforward place to get to. For you, the nearest international airports are Minnesota or Chicago. I don't think you can get a flight from Glasgow to either of them direct. Probably best to fly from Glasgow via Amsterdam and then Chicago. I'll make arrangements for you from there. Just let me know if you're coming into O'Hare or Midway International.'

Brad nodded. Chicago—some place that he'd heard of. He'd be able to find a flight there. 'I'll get online now. I'll get the quickest flight out that I can. Give me a couple of hours and I'll email you back the details.'

'No problem, son. See you soon.'

Brad put down the phone. His hands were shaking. He clicked into the rest of the email. There were four photographs. Two pictures of Alison with her baby and two of Melody. She was still his little girl. She had his blond hair and blue eyes. She even had his smile. And if he played his cards right, he would get to see her again.

He quickly dialled another number he had in his phone. A US attorney he'd been put in touch with who specialised in family law. Best to get some advice before he set foot on US soil. The last thing he wanted to do was cause a scene and get deported.

His brain whirring, he opened a travel website to search for flights. Only one from Glasgow. Leaving in six hours. He didn't hesitate. A few clicks and he was booked. He'd already been to the US in the last two years and knew his machine-readable passport meant he didn't need a visa.

This was it—he was finally going to see his daughter again.

Then something else hit him. Cassidy. He had to tell Cassidy.

He looked at the clock. It wouldn't take him long to pack. He groaned as he remembered his Mini still abandoned at the side of the road. He could get a taxi to the airport. But he couldn't leave without speaking to Cassidy first. It took a few minutes to wrap up his call to the lawyer then he pulled on his jogging trousers and trainers. He could run up the hill to the hospital. Cassidy would be on the ward. He could speak to her there.

He remembered that look on her face in the restaurant. She'd worried about this moment. And to be honest, he'd reached the stage that he'd wondered if this would ever happen.

And now it had.

And he had to go.

But he wouldn't go without speaking to Cassidy. Without reassuring her that he would come back for her. He loved his daughter with his whole heart. But he loved Cassidy, too, and he wanted her to be a part of his life. He looked over to the table where he had an array of little gifts organised for her—all to be placed in the pockets of the calendar. He would do that once he got back from the hospital.

First he had to reassure her. First, he had to tell her that he loved her.

'Where is she?'

'Where's who?' Michael was in the middle of drawing up some heparin. 'Who are you looking for?'

'Cassidy, of course!' Who did that big oaf think he would be looking for? He was out of breath, panting. He wasn't really dressed for the cold, with just a T-shirt and tracksuit top in place, and the run up the hill in the biting cold hadn't helped.

Michael's face paled a little. 'Oh, I take it you haven't heard?'

'Haven't heard what?' Brad's frustration was growing by the second.

'Cassidy had to leave. Her gran had a fall in the nursing home and they thought she might have broken her hip. They are taking her to the Wallace Hospital—on the other side of the city. Cassidy left about an hour ago.'

Brad felt the air whoosh out from him. He pulled out his phone and started dialling her number. But it connected directly to her voice mail.

'Not supposed to use that in here,' muttered Michael.

Brad grabbed his arm. 'How far away is the Wallace? How would I get there at this time of day?' This was the worst possible time for his car to die.

Michael frowned. 'You in a hurry?'

Brad nodded. 'I need to see Cassidy, speak to the boss and arrange a few days off, then get to the airport.'

'You are joking, aren't you?' Michael's eyebrows were raised.

'No. No, I'm not. Give me some directions.'

Michael shook his head. 'At this time of day it will be a bit of a nightmare. You'd need to take the clockwork orange...'

'The what?'

'The underground. That's what we call it around here. You'd need to take the clockwork orange to Cessnock and then get the bus to the hospital. It'll take you about an hour.' He looked at the clock on the wall opposite. 'What time do you need to get to the airport? Because you'll need to get a train to Paisley for that. Then a bus to the airport.'

Brad's head was currently mush. There was no way he was going to get across the city—find Cassidy in a strange hospital, get back, pack and get to the airport in time.

He threw up his hands in frustration and left the hospital, walking back down the hill towards his flat.

He tried her phone again three times and sent her two text messages—but it was obvious she had her phone switched off. What could he do?

He got back home and pulled the biggest suitcase he had from the wardrobe and started throwing things inside. Jeans, jumpers, boots, T-shirts—anything he could think of.

He sat down and tried her phone again. Straight to voice mail. 'Cassidy—it's Brad. I heard about your gran. I'm really sorry and I hope she's okay. I really, really need to speak to you and I don't want to do it over the phone. Please phone me back as soon as you get this message. Please...' He hesitated for a second. 'I love you, Cass.'

He put the phone down. A wave of regret was washing over him. The first time he told her he loved her should have been when he was staring into her big brown eyes—not leaving a message on a phone. But he needed to let her know how he felt. She had to know how much she meant to him.

He looked at the rest of the items on the table. Her flat was only five minutes away— he could go around now and put them in the calendar for her. He could also take some time to write her a letter and explain what had happened. That way, if he didn't get to speak to her, she'd know he'd never meant to leave like this.

He looked at the clock again. Did he really not have the time to get to the other side of the city and back? His heart fell. He knew he didn't. Latest check-in time at the airport was two hours before his flight left. He would never make it. This was the only flight to Chicago that left in the next three days. He had to be on it. The chance to see his daughter again was just too important. He'd waited too long for this moment. He couldn't put this off, no matter how much he wanted to see Cassidy.

He picked up the items from the table and grabbed his keys. He had to try and make this right.

Cassidy leaned back against the wall. The cool hospital concrete was freezing, cutting straight through her thin top, but she welcomed it as she felt completely frazzled. Six hours after she'd got here, her gran was finally being wheeled to Theatre. Her hip was definitely fractured and she was in pain. The orthopaedic surgeon had tried to put her off until the next day, but he hadn't met Cassidy Rae before.

She'd waited until she was sure her gran had disappeared along the corridor to Theatre before she started rummaging around her bag. She badly needed a coffee. Her mobile clattered to the floor as she tried to find her purse.

She picked it up and switched it back on. It had sounded earlier in the A and E department and one of the staff had told her to switch it off. The phone buzzed back into life and started to beep constantly.

Text message from Brad. *'Phone me.'*

Another text message from Brad. *'Phone me as soon as you get this.'*

Text message. *Two voice-mail messages.*

Cassidy felt her heart start to flutter in her chest. She hadn't managed to phone Brad since her gran's accident. Was he worried about her? Or was it something else?

She walked along the corridor and out of the main door, standing to one side and pressing the phone to her ear. She listened to the first message. What on earth was wrong? What didn't he want to say on the phone? Her brain started to panic so much she almost missed the end of the message. *'I love you.'*

Brad had just told her he loved her. On

the phone. And while she wanted the warm feeling to spread throughout her body, she couldn't help feeling something was wrong. His voice—the tone of it.

Had something happened to him? She pressed for the next message.

*'Cassidy, honey, I'm so sorry. I really wanted to speak to you. I've left you a letter at home—it explains everything. I will be back, I promise. And I'll phone you as soon as I get there. And I'll email you as soon as I get near a computer. I love you, Cassidy.'*

Get back from where? Her fingers scrolled for his name and pressed 'dial'. It rang and then diverted to voice mail. His phone must be switched off.

Where was he?

Her agitation was rising. She didn't need this right now. Her gran was in Theatre. She should be concentrating on that. And he should be here with her, helping her through this. Where was he?

She sent him a quick text. *'Still at hospital with Gran. What's going on? Won't be home for a few hours.'*

Maybe he'd been called into work again? Maybe that was it. But something inside her didn't agree.

She walked back inside. There was nothing

she could do right now. She had to stay here and be with her gran. There was no telling how she'd be when she woke from her anaesthetic. Cassidy wanted to be close.

And no matter how much she wanted to know what was going on with Brad, he'd just have to wait.

# CHAPTER NINE

*20 December*

THE alarm sounded and Cassidy groaned and thumped the reset button with her hand. Even stretching out from under the warm duvet for a second was too cold. She heard a little muffled sound and seconds later felt a little draught at the bottom of the duvet.

Bert. The alarm had woken him and he was cold, too, so he'd sneaked into the bottom of her bed just as he'd done for the last ten days.

Ten days. Two hundred and forty hours— no, it had actually been forty-seven hours since she'd last spoken to Brad.

Sometimes when she woke in the morning—just for a millisecond—she thought everything was all right again. But then she remembered he was gone, searching for his daughter in North-blooming-Woods, Wisconsin. She'd had to look the place up on the internet—she didn't even know where it was.

By the time she'd got back from the hospital that night, Brad's flight had been in the air for four hours. He was long gone.

And although it helped just a little that he'd tried to contact her and that he'd left her a letter, it didn't take away from the fact that he'd gone. Just like that. At the drop of a hat.

She knew she was being unreasonable. He'd waited nearly two years to find his daughter—of course he should go. But her heart wasn't as rational as her head tried to be.

Her heart was broken in two.

What if he never came back? What if the only way he could have contact with his daughter was to stay in Wisconsin? What if he fell back in love with Melody's mother?

Every irrational thought in the world had circulated in her mind constantly for the last ten days and nights. Even Bert wasn't helping.

He kept looking at the door and sniffing around Brad's shoes in the hope he would reappear again.

She had to be the unluckiest woman in the world. Twice Brad had phoned her mobile— and both times she had missed his call. Both times she'd been working and both times she'd been with a patient.

He'd phoned the ward one day but she hadn't been on duty. And when he'd phoned the flat she'd been visiting her gran, who was still in hospital.

Every time she tried to call him back she'd received an 'unobtainable' signal.

He'd warned her. He'd warned her that North Woods was aptly named, surrounded by thick woods and hills with poor reception for mobiles and internet connections.

He'd sent two emails letting her know that he'd contacted a family lawyer and made contact with Alison. After some fraught negotiations he'd been allowed supervised access to see Melody twice. They were currently stuck in the land of legal mumbo-jumbo, trying to figure out the parental rights of two Australians in the US. Alison was covered—she'd married an American. But Brad's position was more difficult, particularly when he was officially only on 'holiday'.

It didn't help that his lawyer was advising him to look at extradition since Melody had been removed from Australia without permission.

She really, really wanted to talk to him.

She wanted to hear his voice, feel his arms

around her, feel his body pressed next to hers. Particularly now. A warm dog around her feet might be nice, but it just didn't cut it.

She didn't even feel festive any more. Her favourite time of year had been blighted by the fact the man she loved was on the other side of the Atlantic. The flight had taken fourteen hours to reach Chicago, and then another few for the air transfer to North Woods. It wasn't exactly the easiest place to get to. And it wouldn't be the easiest place to get home from either.

But as soon as he did, she knew what she was going to do. She knew what she was going to say. This forced separation had clarified everything for her. She'd made up her mind.

Now all she could do was wait.

Brad's heart was in his mouth. His little girl seemed completely unfazed by him. Alison was another matter entirely.

Ten days of trying to keep his temper in check. Ten days of biting back all the things he really, really wanted to say.

Once she'd got over the initial shock, Alison had been shamed into a visit at his lawyer's office. She'd brought her husband along, who seemed equally outraged that Brad had dared to appear into their lives in North Woods, Wisconsin.

It hadn't taken long for his lawyer to go through the legal aspects of removing a child from another country without parental consent. Alison's lawyer had been surprisingly quiet and encouraged his client to agree in principle to some short supervised access spells.

He'd been here ten days and had spent three hours with his daughter.

He'd also spent innumerable hours trying to contact Cassidy back home.

Home? Scotland?

In Brad's mind right now, home was wherever Cassidy was. Wherever they could be together. He wanted to spend hours on the phone to her, talking through things with her and telling her how he felt.

But North Woods didn't seem to be a place with normal communication methods in mind—and to be fair, Joe, his private detective, had warned him about this. In theory, he would have managed to co-ordinate time differences, shift patterns and visiting schedules. But reality was much harder. Right now it seemed as if an old-fashioned carrier pigeon would be more effective than modern-day technology.

He glanced at his watch. Time for another visit. Time to see his gorgeous blonde, curly-headed daughter, who could skim stones across the lake like a professional. Time to get the wheels in motion to learn about more permanent types of access. Time to set up an agreed method of communication between them all. One that meant he could talk to his beautiful daughter without having to face the minefield that was her mother.

Time to get his life in order.

## 22 December

A Christmas bride. That's what smelly-cat woman had told her. Was there any chance she could go and demand her twenty quid back?

Right now it felt as if she'd been conned. False pretences. That's what they called it. But she'd never heard of a fortune-teller being sued. Just as well she'd never believed any of it.

Cassidy tugged her thick black boots on, trying to ignore the trickle of water inside that instantly soaked through her sock. There was about three feet of snow outside. It had been the same last night when she'd come home from work.

If she'd been organised—or cared enough—she would have stuffed her already soaked boots with newspaper and stuck them under the radiator. Instead, she'd flung them across the room and fallen into bed instantly.

She couldn't even be bothered to prepare something to eat. Her cupboards were a disgrace. Oh, if she wanted chocolate or crisps or bakery items like chocolate éclairs or cupcakes, she was fine. If she wanted anything substantial to eat, she was well and truly snookered.

Cassidy pulled on a cardigan, her gran's red wool coat and a black furry hat. It shouldn't take too long to get up the hill to the hospital. Her only problem would be if the pavement hadn't been gritted. Yesterday she'd picked up three people who'd slipped, trying to climb the hill, and caught another as he'd almost slid past her.

Maybe a coffee would help? A skinny caramel latte would be perfect.

She gave Bert a pat on the way out—even he was too intelligent to want to go out in this weather.

The cold air instantly stung her cheeks. Snow was starting to fall again already. Within a few hours there could easily be another few feet on the ground. Getting home again would be a nightmare.

The aroma caught her. The smell of a freshly prepared caramel latte. She closed her eyes. Heaven on earth.

'Cassidy?'

The voice stopped her in her tracks. It was quiet. Like a question. Unsure, uncertain.

'Brad!'

She didn't hesitate. She didn't care who was in the street around them. She didn't worry about the slippery pavement covered in snow beneath her feet. She launched herself at him.

'Oof...'

He fell backwards and the latte he'd been carrying toppled, leaving a trail of pale brown on the white snow.

'Why didn't you tell me you were coming home? When did you arrive? Do you know how many times I tried to phone you? What on earth is wrong with that place? Why can't you get a decent signal there? And how dare you tell me you love me in a message?' She finished by slapping her gloved hand on his chest. Her knees pinned him to the ground beneath her.

All he could see was her face. Her curls were escaping from the sides of the black furry hat and her cheeks were tinged with red. A face that he'd longed to see for the last twelve days. It looked perfect.

He lifted his head from the snow. 'Is this a happy-to-see-me greeting or a mad-as-hell greeting?'

She furrowed her brow for a second then she broke into a smile and bent towards him, kissing the tip of his nose. 'What do you think?'

His head sagged back against the snow. 'Thank goodness.' He moved underneath her. 'Can I get up now?'

Her grin spread from ear to ear as she turned her head sideways and noticed people staring at them lying on the pavement. 'I suppose so.'

He stood up and brushed the snow from his back. 'I've missed you,' he said as he wrapped his arm around her shoulders.

'Me, too.'

'Can we go inside?'

'Yes, I mean no. I want to do something first. I promised myself I would do something the next time I saw you. Come with me.' She grabbed his hand, waiting until he'd grabbed the handle of his wheeled suitcase and pulled him across the road.

'Sounds ominous. Where are we going?'

'You'll see.'

She walked quickly along the road, in her excitement almost forgetting he was pulling a heavy suitcase through snow. But in a few moments she stopped and smiled. 'In here,' she said.

He looked around him, puzzled by the surroundings. They'd moved away from the busy street to a small church with an even smaller cemetery, virtually hidden from the road. Its tiny spire was the only thing that made it noticeable among the surrounding buildings.

'I didn't even know this was here.'

'Lots of people don't. But two hundred years ago this was one of the main roads into Glasgow.'

He waited while she pushed open an iron gate and walked behind the railings. He followed her in. totally bemused.

'What on earth are we doing here? Is this the church you normally go to? You've never mentioned it.' He looked around at the old worn gravestones. Some of the writing was barely visible now, washed away through time, wind, rain and grime. 'Looks like no one's been buried here in a very long time.'

Cassidy nodded and pulled him under one of the trees. All of a sudden her rose-tinged cheeks looked pale. He could feel the tremors in her skin under her coat. The snow was starting to coat the fur on her hat in a white haze.

Her voice was shaking as she started to speak. 'You told me you loved me.'

He clasped his hands around her. 'And I do, Cassidy. I didn't want to tell you like that, but things happened so quickly and I didn't want you to think I'd just walked away. I wanted you to know how I felt about you. I wanted you to know that I was definitely coming back.' His voice tailed off.

'I didn't want you to think I was abandoning you.' It was so important to him. To tell her that he wasn't like Bobby or her parents. To tell her that he would never abandon her. That he wanted to be with her for ever.

Her eyes were glazed with hidden tears, but she didn't look unhappy. Just very determined.

'What is it, Cassidy? What's wrong?'

'I was wrong. When I spoke to you about Christmas and its traditions and not leaving Scotland—I was wrong.'

The cold air was making her breath come out in a steam. Short blasts.

'You were right when you said it was about the people—or person—you spend it with.' Her eyes swept around them, taking in the ancient church and graveyard. 'I love Scotland. You know I love Scotland. But I love you more and I want to be wherever you are.'

Brad blinked, snowflakes getting in his eyes. A two-hour flight, followed by another fourteen-hour flight, all worrying about Cassidy. How she would be, whether she would forgive him for leaving without saying goodbye, whether she would be angry with him. 'You love me,' he said slowly, his sense of relief sending a flood of warm blood through his chilled skin.

She nodded, the smile on her face reaching right up into her brown eyes.

'You love me,' he said again.

'Yes, yes, I love you. Do you want me to shout it out loud?' Her voice rose, sending some birds fluttering from the tree above.

He bent his head and kissed her. Taking her sweet lips against his own, pulling her close to him, keeping out all the cold that surrounded them. He'd wanted to do nothing else for the last twelve days. Twelve days and twelve long nights without Cassidy in his arms had driven him crazy.

'How do you feel about fourteen-hour flights?' he whispered.

She pulled backwards a little, nodding slowly. 'To North Woods, Wisconsin?' She reached up, pulling her hand from her red leather glove and running her finger down the side of his cheek. 'I think that's something we can do together.'

He sucked in a breath. She was prepared to go with him to see his daughter. She was prepared to meet the challenge of their life together. She'd come full circle. Just like he had. Eighteen months ago he couldn't have been lower. Cassidy had lit up his world in every way possible. He couldn't imagine life without her.

A shiver stole down his spine. He nuzzled into her neck. 'You've still not told me, what are we doing here, Cass?'

He watched her take a deep breath. She looked at him steadily. 'I've decided I'm a modern woman and want to embrace life— in every way possible. I've always loved this place—especially in the winter.' She swept her arm across the scene. 'How do you feel about this as a wedding setting?'

Brad froze. She hadn't. She hadn't just said that, had she?

She looked terrified. Now that the words were out, she looked as if she could faint on the spot.

'Did you just propose?' He lifted his eyebrow at her in disbelief.

'I think so.' She trembled.

He picked her up and spun her around. 'Isn't this supposed to be my job? Aren't I supposed to go down on one knee and propose to you with a single red rose and a diamond ring?' He pressed his face next to hers, his lips connecting with hers again.

'You were taking too long,' she mumbled. 'It took you a full month to kiss me. What chance did I have?' She hesitated. 'So what do you think?' There was fear in her voice, still that little piece of uncertainty.

'I think you should look in pocket twenty-four of your calendar.'

'What?' She looked momentarily stunned. Not the answer she was expecting.

Cassidy's brain was desperately trying to click into gear. She'd just asked the biggest question in her life. What kind of an answer was that? She hadn't looked at the calendar since the night Brad had left—she'd just assumed he wouldn't have had a chance to fill it before he'd gone.

He set her feet down on the ground. The grin on his face spread from ear to ear, his head, shoulders and eyelashes covered in snowflakes. 'Well, I'm not entirely a modern man. This is my job.' He dropped to one knee on the snow-covered grass. 'So much for taking too long—let's just cut right to the chase. Cassidy Rae, will you do me the honour of being my wife? Will you promise to love, honour and keep me, in sickness and in health, for as long as we both shall live?'

She dropped to her knees beside him. 'That's not a proposal.' She looked stunned. 'That's a wedding vow.'

'That's okay,' he whispered, pulling her even closer. 'I've already got the wedding ring.'

Her eyes widened. 'Pocket twenty-four?'

He nodded. 'Pocket twenty-four. I didn't know there was a church around here. I was hoping that we could say our own vows.'

She giggled. 'Looks like I'm going to be a Christmas bride after all.'

He looked completely confused. 'What on earth are you talking about?'

She smiled. 'Well, one day I might tell you a little story...'

# EPILOGUE

*One year later*

'YOU'VE got to pick the best stones, Cassidy. They need to be flat on both sides.' The blue eyes regarded her seriously before the little face broke into a broad smile. 'That's why I always win,' she whispered, giving a conspiratorial glance over her shoulder towards Brad, who was standing at the lakeside waiting for them both.

'What's going on with my girls?' he shouted.

Melody held her gloved hand out towards Cassidy as they walked back over to Brad.

Cassidy looked down at the blonde curls spilling out from the green woolly hat. She gave Brad a smile. This was their third visit to North Woods, Wisconsin, and Brad had finally been allowed some unsupervised access to his child. Melody was a loving, easy child who, luckily enough, seemed totally oblivious to the tensions between her natural parents.

She spoke to Brad online every week and had been happy to meet Cassidy, loving the fact that her dad had a Scottish wife. She'd even painted Cassidy a picture of them all living in a Scottish castle.

Cassidy winked at Brad. 'Melody and I needed some time to make our plan. We think we've found a sixer.'

'A sixer? What on earth is that?' He shook his head in amusement at them both.

Melody's voice piped up. 'You should know what a sixer is, Daddy.' The stone-skimming champion looked at him seriously, holding up the flat grey stone in her hand like an winning prize. 'This stone will skim across the water *six* times before it goes under.'

'Aha.' He knelt down beside her, touching the stone with his finger, 'A sixer? Really?' He shook his head and folded him arm across his chest. 'No way. Not that stone.'

'It really is, Daddy.'

Brad's face broke into a big smile as he straightened up and slung his arm around Cassidy's shoulder. 'Prove it.'

They watched as Melody took her position at the lakeside edge, narrowing her gaze and pulling her hand back to her shoulder. She let out a yell as she released the stone, sending it skimming over the flat water, bouncing across the lake.

Cassidy leaned against Brad's shoulder. 'One, two, three, four, five, six. Your daughter was absolutely right. It was a sixer. Now, where does she get that skill from, I wonder?'

He laughed. 'Her dad, definitely her dad. I could throw a mean ball as a kid.'

He picked up Melody, who was shrieking over her success. 'What a star!' he shouted as he threw her into the air, catching her in his arms and spinning her round.

Cassidy pulled her red wool coat further around her, trying to ward off the biting cold. North Woods was nearly as cold as Glasgow at this time of year.

Brad came over and whispered in her ear. 'Happy anniversary, Mrs Donovan.' His cold nose was pressed against her cheek as he wrapped his arms around her waist.

Cassidy felt herself relax against him. After all her worries, all her stresses, things had worked out just fine. They'd married two weeks after his proposal in the churchyard— as quickly as they legally could.

Her gran had recovered quickly from her broken hip and recuperated back in the nursing home with some expert care. She was on a new drug trial, and although her Alzheimer's hadn't improved, it certainly hadn't got any worse. The relief for Cassidy was that the episodes of aggression seemed to have abated. She still visited her gran as often as possible but she was confident in the care the nursing home provided.

That had given her the freedom she'd needed to join Brad on a two-month visit to Australia and on three trips to the States to see Melody.

After a few tense months, Alison's lawyer had finally talked some sense into his client and visiting rights had been sorted out. It meant that every few months they could have Melody for a week at a time to stay with them.

Brad had looked at a few jobs nearby and been interviewed for a position at the local hospital. Cassidy had just seen an ad for a specialist nurse to help set up an anticoagulant clinic and knew it was just what she was looking for. There was only one more thing that could make this perfect.

She turned round and put her arms around his neck. 'Happy anniversary, Dr Donovan.' She kissed him on his cold lips.

'So how do you feel about North Woods,

Wisconsin?' he asked, his smile reaching from one ear to the other.

Cassidy looked over her shoulder at the lake with ice around the edges and thick trees surrounding it. 'I think it has potential.' She smiled.

He raised his eyebrows. 'Potential? Potential for what?'

He was waiting. Waiting to see what she would say. He didn't know she'd just found an ad for her dream job. He didn't know that there had been a message from the hospital after he'd left to collect Melody, offering him the job he'd just been interviewed for. But all of that could wait. Right now she wanted the chance to still surprise her new husband.

She rose up on the tips of her toes and whispered in his ear, 'I think North Woods, Wisconsin might be a nice place to make a baby.'

His jaw dropped and his eyes twinkled as he picked her up and spun her round. 'You know, Mrs Donovan, I think you could be right.'

\* \* \* \* \*